TO BLAME THEM
DI SAM COBBS
BOOK THIRTEEN

M A COMLEY

Copyright © 2024 by M A Comley

All rights reserved.

No part of this book may be reproduced in any form or by any electronic or mechanical means, including information storage and retrieval systems, without written permission from the author, except for the use of brief quotations in a book review.

Thank you once again to Clive Rowlandson for allowing me to use one of his stunning photos for the cover.

ALSO BY M A COMLEY

Blind Justice (Novella)

Cruel Justice (Book #1)

Mortal Justice (Novella)

Impeding Justice (Book #2)

Final Justice (Book #3)

Foul Justice (Book #4)

Guaranteed Justice (Book #5)

Ultimate Justice (Book #6)

Virtual Justice (Book #7)

Hostile Justice (Book #8)

Tortured Justice (Book #9)

Rough Justice (Book #10)

Dubious Justice (Book #11)

Calculated Justice (Book #12)

Twisted Justice (Book #13)

Justice at Christmas (Short Story)

Prime Justice (Book #14)

Heroic Justice (Book #15)

Shameful Justice (Book #16)

Immoral Justice (Book #17)

Toxic Justice (Book #18)

Overdue Justice (Book #19)

Unfair Justice (a 10,000 word short story)

Irrational Justice (a 10,000 word short story)

Seeking Justice (a 15,000 word novella)

Caring For Justice (a 24,000 word novella)
Savage Justice (a 17,000 word novella)
Justice at Christmas #2 (a 15,000 word novella)
Gone in Seconds (Justice Again series #1)
Ultimate Dilemma (Justice Again series #2)
Shot of Silence (Justice Again series #3)
Taste of Fury (Justice Again series #4)
Crying Shame (Justice Again series #5)
See No Evil (Justice Again #6)
To Die For (DI Sam Cobbs #1)
To Silence Them (DI Sam Cobbs #2)
To Make Them Pay (DI Sam Cobbs #3)
To Prove Fatal (DI Sam Cobbs #4)
To Condemn Them (DI Sam Cobbs #5)
To Punish Them (DI Sam Cobbs #6)
To Entice Them (DI Sam Cobbs #7)
To Control Them (DI Sam Cobbs #8)
To Endanger Lives (DI Sam Cobbs #9)
To Hold Responsible (DI Sam Cobbs #10)
To Catch a Killer (DI Sam Cobbs #11)
To Believe The Truth (DI Sam Cobbs #12)
To Blame Them (DI Sam Cobbs #13)
To Judge Them (DI Sam Cobbs #14)
Forever Watching You (DI Miranda Carr thriller)
Wrong Place (DI Sally Parker thriller #1)
No Hiding Place (DI Sally Parker thriller #2)
Cold Case (DI Sally Parker thriller#3)
Deadly Encounter (DI Sally Parker thriller #4)

Lost Innocence (DI Sally Parker thriller #5)
Goodbye My Precious Child (DI Sally Parker #6)
The Missing Wife (DI Sally Parker #7)
Truth or Dare (DI Sally Parker #8)
Where Did She Go? (DI Sally Parker #9)
Sinner (DI Sally Parker #10)
The Good Die Young (DI Sally Parker #11)
Coping Without You (DI Sally Parker #12)
Could It Be Him? (DI Sally Parker #13)
Web of Deceit (DI Sally Parker Novella)
The Missing Children (DI Kayli Bright #1)
Killer On The Run (DI Kayli Bright #2)
Hidden Agenda (DI Kayli Bright #3)
Murderous Betrayal (Kayli Bright #4)
Dying Breath (Kayli Bright #5)
Taken (DI Kayli Bright #6)
The Hostage Takers (DI Kayli Bright Novella)
No Right to Kill (DI Sara Ramsey #1)
Killer Blow (DI Sara Ramsey #2)
The Dead Can't Speak (DI Sara Ramsey #3)
Deluded (DI Sara Ramsey #4)
The Murder Pact (DI Sara Ramsey #5)
Twisted Revenge (DI Sara Ramsey #6)
The Lies She Told (DI Sara Ramsey #7)
For The Love Of... (DI Sara Ramsey #8)
Run for Your Life (DI Sara Ramsey #9)
Cold Mercy (DI Sara Ramsey #10)
Sign of Evil (DI Sara Ramsey #11)

Indefensible (DI Sara Ramsey #12)

Locked Away (DI Sara Ramsey #13)

I Can See You (DI Sara Ramsey #14)

The Kill List (DI Sara Ramsey #15)

Crossing The Line (DI Sara Ramsey #16)

Time to Kill (DI Sara Ramsey #17)

Deadly Passion (DI Sara Ramsey #18)

Son Of The Dead (DI Sara Ramsey #19)

Evil Intent (DI Sara Ramsey #20)

The Games People Play (DI Sara Ramsey #21)

Revenge Streak (DI Sara Ramsey #22)

Seeking Retribution (DI Sara Ramsey #23)

Gone… But Where? (DI Sara Ramsey #24)

I Know The Truth (A Psychological thriller)

She's Gone (A psychological thriller)

Shattered Lives (A psychological thriller)

Evil In Disguise – a novel based on True events

Deadly Act (Hero series novella)

Torn Apart (Hero series #1)

End Result (Hero series #2)

In Plain Sight (Hero Series #3)

Double Jeopardy (Hero Series #4)

Criminal Actions (Hero Series #5)

Regrets Mean Nothing (Hero series #6)

Prowlers (Hero Series #7)

Sole Intention (Intention series #1)

Grave Intention (Intention series #2)

Devious Intention (Intention #3)

Cozy mysteries

Murder at the Wedding

Murder at the Hotel

Murder by the Sea

Death on the Coast

Death By Association

Merry Widow (A Lorne Simpkins short story)

It's A Dog's Life (A Lorne Simpkins short story)

A Time To Heal (A Sweet Romance)

A Time For Change (A Sweet Romance)

High Spirits

The Temptation series (Romantic Suspense/New Adult Novellas)

Past Temptation

Lost Temptation

Clever Deception (co-written by Linda S Prather)

Tragic Deception (co-written by Linda S Prather)

Sinful Deception (co-written by Linda S Prather)

ACKNOWLEDGMENTS

Special thanks as always go to @studioenp for their superb cover design expertise.

My heartfelt thanks go to my wonderful editor Emmy, and my proofreaders Joseph and Barbara for spotting all the lingering nits.

Thank you also to my amazing ARC Group who help to keep me sane during this process.

RIP Mum, you've taken a huge part of my heart with you. Some days are definitely more difficult than others.

To Mary, gone, but never forgotten. I hope you found the peace you were searching for my dear friend. I miss you each and every day.

PROLOGUE

Steven Cox was weary, had been for months. This was the last thing he needed, to be summoned to his boss' office, midway through his shift. He wound his way through the storeroom to the room at the end of the corridor and tapped on the door. It was a feeble knock; he half wished that Mr White hadn't heard it, which would mean he could go back to work, but he was wrong. The door was wrenched open, and Mr White stood there, in all his glory, his large belly straining the buttons on his blue shirt. The sleeves of his jacket finishing three inches higher than his wrist. His face bright red with anger, that much was indisputable.

"You're late. If I give you a time for you to attend, you damn well make sure you show up here on time, got that?"

"Sorry, sir. I got waylaid by a customer asking me in which aisle the light bulbs could be found. As per your instructions, I took the lady to the correct place instead of just telling her they were in aisle six."

White huffed out a breath and rolled his eyes. "Yes, yes. You're here now. Come in and take a seat."

He stood to one side, allowing Mr White to get behind his

desk first before he sat down himself as the office was on the small side.

White cleared his throat and looked him in the eye. "It's been brought to my attention by your supervisor that your work this week has been... how shall I say this? Ah, yes, on the lacklustre side. Even your colleagues, who work alongside you every day, are struggling to keep up the pretence any longer."

Steven's gaze dropped to his slender hands, wringing in his lap. He remained quiet. It was useless putting his point across. White had never listened in the past, why should today be any different?

"Are you listening to me? Don't you have anything to say in your defence?"

He glanced up and met White's gaze again. "What would be the point, sir? You've never listened to a word I've said in the past, why should it be any different today?"

White was clearly angered by his rebuttal. He fidgeted in his seat and glared at him. "Any real man would fight for his job."

His boss's words stung, but all he could do was shrug because it was the truth. He was no longer a real man. There was very little, if any, fight left in him these days. His two boys would vouch for him on that count. Now that his wife was gone, he didn't have a purpose in this life.

"Haven't you got anything to say for yourself?"

Steven shrugged again. "Not really. Would you listen if I gave you a ton of excuses?"

"Unlikely. Okay, then you leave me no other option than to give you a month's notice as per your contract. I'm sorry, but the rest of the staff have all complained that they appear to be carrying you, that they've been doing that for the last six months. Let's face it, this isn't your first warning, it's your third. I've given you a fair crack of the whip. More chances than any other member of staff, but it counts for nothing, does it? You're determined to keep wallowing in self-pity, even after all these months. While I'm sorry your wife died, it was very sad for you and your boys, there comes a time when you have to put tragic events in the past and move on with your life."

Tears filled Steven's eyes. "If you say so," he mumbled, avoiding eye contact with his boss.

"Okay, you're free to go. There's no need for you to finish your shift today, you've been less than useless all day, all week, in fact. Go home and get some rest. Have you been sleeping?"

A glimmer of concern emerged that Steven hadn't been expecting.

"No, I rarely sleep these days."

"Have you been to the doctor?"

"Yes, last month. He gave me a pot of anti-depressants and a packet of sleeping pills."

"And have you taken them?"

"No. I don't want to start on that slippery slope. I have the children to consider," he replied. He thought he was saying what White wanted to hear, hoping against hope that his boss would show him some sympathy.

White, however, was having none of it. "Well, if you're not prepared to listen to the professionals there's very little anyone around here can do for you. Get your life back on track, Cox, if only for the sake of your two sons."

"I'm trying, believe me. It's not as easy as people think it is."

"What about the boys? Are they still cut up about losing their mother?"

"Yes, they're quiet and withdrawn. I feel responsible but I haven't got it in me to do anything about it."

White clenched his fist and thumped it on the desk. "My

God, have you heard yourself? Those boys are relying on you to see them through these dark times."

"I know that. I don't need to be reminded. Stop stating the obvious. It's all right for you, sitting there in your executive chair without a care in the world."

"I can assure you, that's not the case at all. My wife is away at the moment, caring for her mother who is eighty-six and fading fast from dementia. We haven't seen each other in two months; it's called life. Everyone has problems and needs to knuckle down at times to overcome issues that have been flung at them."

Steven held his head in shame and muttered, "I'm sorry. I had no idea you were going through that."

"And do you know why that is?"

"No."

"Because I leave my problems at home. The minute I step into my office, I put my professional head on. It's what we have to do as adults to get by. Life is never a bed of roses, God is always testing us. I remember my father sitting me down when I lost my mother, when I was in my teens, and telling me that 'life is a challenge with many obstacles that we need to conquer'. He was right. You see, we have more in common than you think we have. I just choose to leave my problems at home and make the most of my time at work. I find it fulfilling. You need to get your head and your heart sorted out, if only for the boys' sakes. Will you do that for me?"

Steven sighed. "If only it were that simple."

"It is. Take my word for it. Are you a man or a mouse? Because from where I'm sitting, I think the latter is probably true. You need to go home and give yourself a good talking-to. I agree with you on one point, I would ditch those pills, they've never done anyone any good, not really. They hook you, make you reliant on them. Damn things can turn your world upside down, although, by the look of things, it's that way already. Have you considered talking to anyone? A counsellor perhaps?"

"I've thought about it. The doctor advised me to get in touch with Cruse, but they're rushed off their feet, answering calls from people who really need their help."

"Stop right there. You're one of those people, whether you want to admit it or not. Give them a call today, go on a waiting list if you have to. I repeat, this shouldn't be about you, you should be putting your boys first."

Fresh tears filled Steven's eyes, and he nodded. "I'll do it. Thank you."

"Going back to what I said at the start of this conversation, if you're willing to change your ways, I'll reconsider giving you your cards. It's up to you to prove me wrong and kick yourself up the backside. Will you?"

"I'll try. That's as much as I can say right now."

"Get yourself home, spend some time with your lads and come back tomorrow equipped with a better attitude. What do you say?"

"I'm going to give it a shot."

"Good. Cox, my door is always open. I know it's not the done thing for a man to admit when he needs help, but you're going to need to swallow that pride of yours and seek it out."

"Thank you, sir. Is that all now?"

"It is. Enjoy the rest of your day."

Steven resisted the temptation to roll his eyes. *What was there to enjoy?*

"Get out there, in the open air, have a good walk. That's supposed to be the key to combatting mental health issues these days, isn't it? You know, since we were forced to endure lockdown."

"I might just do that. Thanks for being so understanding, Mr White."

"I'll see you in the morning."

Steven left the office and headed straight for his locker. His supervisor, Mr Hayes, was lingering in the area.

"Hello, sir. I'm going home for the day."

"Good. How did it go in there?"

"I've been given my cards with an added caveat that if I come back tomorrow with a different mental attitude, Mr White will be willing to reconsider giving me the sack."

Hayes patted him on the shoulder. "I'm sorry it has come to this, Steven, you left me no option. The rest of the staff have been carrying you for months now, and they're sick of it."

"I know. Pass on my thanks to them, none of this was intentional. I hope the death of a loved one doesn't blight their lives or yours anytime soon. All I can tell you is that it's debilitating. It eats away at you, despite you trying to do all you can to combat it."

"We've all lost a loved one over the years, it's part of life and we need to deal with it, mate. You're not the only man to have ever lost his wife to cancer. You should have reached out to us, let us know how much you were struggling. I know a certain young lady who would have taken you under her wing if you'd given her the chance."

He cringed, knowing who he was talking about. The thought of that gross woman coming near him and his kids made him retch.

"Are you all right?"

"No, I'm sick of all this. Of you standing there, dismissing the loss of my wife as if I'd had a tooth knocked out during a game of football. Have some compassion, man. Either that or stay the hell away from me."

"Charming, I was only trying to offer you some advice. I'll keep my mouth shut next time."

"You do that. I'm going home."

Hayes turned his back without saying anything further. Steven regretted his actions, but seconds later he was walking out of the DIY store's rear entrance and getting into his car with another thought running through his mind.

AFTER STOPPING off for a swift walk around the park close to his house, he drove home and put the car in the garage then stepped inside the house and searched for a pen and paper. He spent the next thirty minutes pouring his soul out on two sheets of an A5 pad until he heard a key being inserted into the front door. He tucked the pad under the cushion and met the boys in the hallway.

"Jesus, Dad, you scared us. Where's the car?"

"I had to drop it off for repairs at the local garage," he lied.

"Why are you home early?" Josh, his eldest son asked.

"I was told I could leave early so that I could spend some time with my boys."

"Oh, that's nice, but we've got a mountain of homework to get through. We're going to make a start now."

"All right, son. What do you fancy for tea? Fish fingers or chicken dippers, that's the choice for tonight, until I can get to the supermarket to top up the fridge with fresh veg."

Josh raised an eyebrow. "Like it matters. That stuff usually sits in the fridge until it goes off. You normally only buy it for show."

Josh and his brother, Ben, removed their shoes in the hallway and traipsed up the stairs.

"Hey, don't you guys want a drink and a snack?"

"We used the last of the milk for our cereals this morning,

and I doubt if you thought about stopping off at the shops on the way home, did you?" Josh shouted over his shoulder.

"Shit. Okay, I'll remedy that now and go to the shop on the corner. Give me fifteen minutes."

"Whatever," both boys said in unison.

Steven checked his wallet to see how much cash he had—very little—and he knew he had almost reached his limit with his bank card as well. He tore into the kitchen and raided the jar in which his wife used to put the utility money away every month. He found a solitary five-pound note in there. "It's better than nothing. Probably won't get me very far, not these days."

He was right, too. The corner shop had recently been taken over by a Greek man, and the prices had gone through the roof. Nearly three quid for four pints of milk, double what it was the last time he'd bought some at the shop under the previous owner, although that was a few years ago. He wished he had the option of going elsewhere, but he didn't, not within walking distance.

Steven gave the robbing shopkeeper his fiver, which covered the milk and the two packets of biscuits he'd picked up as a treat for the boys and walked home again. The rain battered him during his journey. He dashed through the front door and shook off the excess before hanging his jacket up in the hallway. "I'm back, kids. Will milk and biscuits do for you?"

Neither of the boys responded. He went through to the kitchen and plucked a couple of glasses from the cupboard and two side plates from the draining board. He put four biscuits on each of the plates and ferried them upstairs on the wooden tray his wife had bought the week before she'd passed away. It was the final item she'd purchased and was a constant reminder to him.

"Thanks," Josh mumbled, not looking up from his books.

Ben was lying on his stomach on his bed, his books laid out to the side and in front of him.

"How's it going?" Steven asked.

Ben slammed his books shut the second he caught Steven sneaking a peek at them. "Dad. Do you have to snoop?"

Steven placed the milk and biscuits on the bedside cabinet and retreated from the room, feeling utterly dejected. He returned to the lounge and searched for his pad and pen again, knowing the boys would be distracted for at least another hour, then he'd need to get on with sorting out their dinner.

It took him a while to get back into the zone and pick up where he'd left off. He blocked out the thought of Josh and Ben gate-crashing his pity party and set about putting his true feelings down on paper. An hour later, a thump sounded overhead. He shoved the pen and paper back under the cushion and walked into the kitchen to start on the dinner. He removed fish fingers, chips and peas from the freezer and cursed when he discovered there was only enough left for the boys. He checked the veg rack and found a withered old potato with dozens of extra eyes. It would have to do. He gave it a quick wash under the tap, pierced it with a knife and put it on the dirty glass plate in the microwave for six minutes. Then he checked to see if there was a tin of baked beans in the cupboard and a block of cheese in the fridge. He was out of luck with the cheese. *Jacket spud and beans it is then.*

The boys appeared five minutes later and made themselves comfortable at the table. He opened the oven door to see how the food was cooking and cursed under his breath. He'd forgotten to switch it on in his haste to sort out his own dinner, putting himself before his boys.

"Sorry, I'm a dumbwit. Guess who forgot to turn the oven on?"

"Dad!" Ben complained and tipped his chair back as he stood. "I'll be watching TV."

"Yes, that's a good idea. Take the knives and forks in, I'll bring it in to you. My mess-up. The least I can do is let you eat your meals in front of the TV tonight."

"I'll get them," Josh said.

"Is your brother all right?" Steven asked once Ben had left the room.

"We're both fine, Dad. You worry too much."

"It's my job to worry, it's called parenting."

Josh gave him one of his 'whatever' looks and continued to remove the cutlery from the drawer.

He followed his brother into the lounge, and Steven moved towards the back door to peer out of the window at the tip of a back garden. The garden that had once been his wife's pride and joy. Like everything else, he'd let it go to pot over the past six months, since her death. He moved away from yet another painful reminder of the life and love he'd recently lost and checked the contents of the oven again. He removed a pair of tongs from the drawer and turned each of the fish fingers over and shook the chips in the other tin. Another five minutes and he'd be ready to dish up. He lit the gas under the peas and crossed his fingers they'd be cooked in time. He had always been a rubbish cook. Even this simple meal had tested him to his limits. He opened the microwave to see if his potato was cooked, but it wasn't, so he blasted it for another couple of minutes and placed the tin of beans in a saucepan. But his kids would come first. He dished up their meals and delivered them to the lounge.

"Here you go, boys. Do you need anything else?"

Ben muttered something that he didn't quite catch, and Josh nudged him with his knee.

"Come on, Ben, speak up. If you've got something to say, let's have it."

"I haven't."

"Fine. Enjoy your meals. I'm just cooking mine now."

"What? Are you having something different to us?" Josh asked.

"Yes, out of necessity. You had the last of the fingers and chips. I really need to go to the supermarket."

"Hooray, we've been telling you that for ages," Josh replied. He bit into his fish finger and burnt his mouth. "Ouch, this is boiling."

Steven raised an eyebrow. "It's come out of a hot place… you know, the oven. It's always best to test your food before shoving it into your mouth."

"How am I supposed to do that?" Josh queried.

"Think about it, son." Steven went back into the kitchen to hear his beans bubbling away in the pan. "Shit! They're burnt at the bottom now." He shook his head, ashamed of his ability, or lack of, to care for himself and his sons. *How do women always make it look so easy? This cooking lark is harder than it seems. I'm a hopeless twat. Can't even cook baked beans without cocking it up.*

In the end, he managed to salvage most of the beans, but because he had forgotten to turn the potato over halfway through the cooking, the bottom ended up hard and inedible. *What the fuck!*

He ate his meal at the table and regretted his decision when the loneliness hit him with full force. Ben and Josh brought their empty plates out and stacked them in the sink for him to wash. He should have had the balls to tell them to wash up after themselves, but it was another area in which he was lacking. The boys cast his plate a cursory glance, didn't feel the need to whinge about him having a better meal than them because it wasn't, then they returned to the lounge. He cleaned up the kitchen and joined them ten minutes later, only for them to walk out of the room and go back upstairs.

With his stomach half-full, he dozed off in the chair and woke up to find the music of *News at Ten* filling the room. He switched off the TV, checked in on his sons, who were both tucked up in bed with the lights off, and then crawled into bed.

THE NEXT MORNING, he didn't bother getting dressed. Instead, he went downstairs in his pyjamas and made the boys their breakfast. They mumbled a thank you, gathered their bags and left the house.

The quiet destroyed him. He wandered from room to room, worrying if he could go through with his risky plan. An hour later, fully dressed, he did just that.

CHAPTER 1

Detective Inspector Sam Cobbs and her partner, Detective Sergeant Bob Jones, were on their way back to the station after visiting a victim's family. They had briefed the widow and her daughter about what they should expect next, now that their investigation was over and on its way to court. It had been an emotional morning for Sam, who had mistakenly become attached to the two women, against Bob's better judgement.

"Don't say it," she said as she pulled up at the lights on the main road close to the station.

The journey had consisted of silence with the odd sigh from her partner. It was obvious to Sam that he was narked and dying to speak what was on his mind.

"My lips are sealed." He muttered something else without moving his lips, and she groaned.

"You can be a prized dickhead at times. I don't tell you that nearly enough."

He tipped his head back and laughed. "Only when I'm right."

"In your opinion."

"You got too attached to her. Is it any wonder she's been calling you at all hours of the day and night for updates? And another thing, while we're on the subject, when you dish out your business cards you need to stop telling people you're willing to be at their beck and call twenty-four-seven."

"Bollocks. I refuse to do that."

"Why? You're entitled to time off just like the rest of us."

"You're a harsh man, Bob Jones."

"When I need to be. Hey, all I'm doing is looking out for you."

She patted his knee and smiled. "I know and it's appreciated, not needed, but appreciated nevertheless." The lights changed, and she made a left turn. Her mobile rang. "Can you get that for me?"

"If I have to." He removed the phone from the clip on the dashboard. "DI Cobbs' phone. How can I help?"

"Put it on speaker," she whispered.

"Hi, Bob. It's Nick Travis. I know you're out and about at the moment, but I thought you and DI Cobbs might be interested in following up on a call we've just received."

"Hi, Nick, it's Sam. Can you tell us more? We're not far from the station, I'll pull over."

"A woman just rang to say that she and the binman wanted to report something suspicious going on at her neighbour's house. When I sent a patrol out to see what was going on they heard a car running inside the garage and were forced to break down the door to gain entry to the house."

"And what did they find?"

"The owner of the house dead. Looks like he's committed suicide. The pathologist is on his way. I wondered if you'd like to head over there."

"Why not? We've got nothing else on our radar at the moment. It won't take us long to figure out if it is a cut-and-dried case. I'm sure Des won't keep us hanging around too long for his appraisal of the situation."

"Thanks, ma'am. I'll let my guys on the scene know you're on your way." He gave them the address.

"Roger that, Nick." She nodded.

Bob ended the call. "A suicide? We don't usually get involved in them, why the sudden interest in this one?"

"Just going with the flow. Nick's pretty good at assessing situations. I'm willing to go along with him on this one."

"Then so am I. Want me to enter the details into the satnav?"

Sam smiled and pulled out into the traffic again while the machine worked its magic. Thirty-six Fountain Road, Workington, was around ten minutes away from the station, not too far as it turned out.

She drew up outside the semi-detached house, next to Des's van, and they exited the car. Sam produced her warrant card for the officer on duty at the cordon. She recognised him, and he waved it away.

"No need for that, ma'am."

They signed the log, and Sam asked, "Is the pathologist inside?"

"Yes, he's only been here a few minutes himself."

Sam took a few steps closer to the garage. "Des, are you around?"

He poked his head out from the passenger side of the car. "I'm here and I'm warning you now, don't you even consider coming closer without a suit on."

Tutting, she shouted, "Is it necessary?"

Des glared at her.

"It doesn't matter, we'll be right back."

She and Bob returned to the car and donned a white Tyvek suit each. They took a pair of shoe covers with them which they put on immediately outside the garage.

Des came to meet them, his expression stern. "I know you're going to ask what my opinion is on the victim's death, so I'm going to pre-empt you and tell you that I'm not one hundred percent sure this is a suicide, not right now. I'm going to need to carry out a PM before I can give you a definitive answer."

"Fair enough. I'm aware how thorough you like to be. Can you walk us through it?"

He stood aside and gestured for them to join him. "Come into my parlour, and yes, I'm sure you'll find plenty of spiders joining us inside."

Sam scanned the ceiling and the corners of the garage and shuddered. "Okay, let's make this quick."

Des and Bob both laughed.

"You said that intentionally, just to get a reaction out of me, didn't you?"

Des slapped a hand over his chest. "Me? Would I really sink to such levels?"

"You would." She circled the car, her eyes drawn to the victim sitting in the driver's seat. "How old? Around thirty-five to forty?"

"That would be my guesstimate."

"Anyone else in the house?"

"Signs of a family, two sons. Whether they still live here or with their mother remains to be seen. The neighbour next door, Liz Chapman, seems to know a lot about them. She told your colleagues off for breaking the door down because she had a key."

"Eager to get to the victim, were they?"

"You're not wrong."

"I think I would have done the same if I were in their shoes," Bob chipped in, keen to stick up for his colleagues. They had a hard enough job as it was, most of the time.

Sam nodded. "We'll have a word with her afterwards."

Des took up his position on the other side of the car and peered into the passenger side. Sam leaned against the driver's door, allowing Bob the room to make an assessment of the scene himself.

"Nasty. I've never understood why people choose to end their lives this way," Bob said.

"If that's what happened. I'm not convinced but I've yet to discover any signs of foul play to the contrary, either," Des replied.

Sam took in the scene but at this stage had no thoughts either way. She raised her hand to her mouth and coughed, the lingering fumes catching her throat. "I don't think we should hang around in here for too long. Do we know when he was discovered?"

"About nine-thirty or thereabouts."

Sam pushed Bob back to give her space. Being pinned against the car door suddenly made her feel claustrophobic.

"All right, there's no need to push. You could have politely asked me to move," her partner complained.

Sam escaped the garage and sucked in a lungful of clean air before she responded. "Sorry, I just needed to get out of there and get some fresh air. You know my manners are usually impeccable."

"That's debatable at times. Are you all right? I didn't think it was too bad in there."

"You weren't squished into a tiny space, were you?"

"I suppose not. Want me to fetch your bottle of water from the car?"

"No, I'll be fine. Anyway, I think we're done here. We'll nip next door, see what the neighbour has to say. Maybe she'll take pity on us and invite us in for a drink."

"Possibly. Don't you want to have a quick wander around the house first?"

Feeling more at ease now that she'd filled her lungs with

fresher air, she said, "Okay, let's do it." She slipped back into the garage and apologised to Des. "Sorry, not sure what came over me. We're going to have a quick look inside the house, if that's all right with you?"

"Go for it. Let me know if you find anything of interest, won't you?"

"Of course. When will you be carrying out the PM?"

"Later today. Are you going to join me?"

"If you feel there's a need for us to attend then that's what we'll do. In the meantime, we'll have a chat with Mrs Chapman, see if she can shed any light on things."

Sam walked through the internal door that led into the hallway of the house, with Bob close on her heels.

"Shall we stick together?" Bob asked.

Sam peered into the lounge. "No, you see what you can find upstairs. I'll join you once I've had a quick root around down here."

"Suits me."

Bob set off and thumped his way up the stairs and along the landing overhead. Sam switched off, blocking out the heavy-footed lump and concentrated on the family pictures scattered around the room.

Mother, father and two boys, possibly around twelve and fourteen. They all seem happy enough to me.

She studied the parents' eyes to see if she could spot anything lingering in their depths. Nothing as far as she could tell. The room was clutter-free, but she noticed a thick layer of dust on all of the surfaces.

Maybe someone had been ill lately, needing a hospital stay and the housework was the last thing to be considered important.

She wandered into the kitchen next door and immediately took note of what was in the sink. Two cereal bowls and a side plate. She assumed the kids had eaten the cereals and either the wife or the husband had eaten a round or two of toast, judging by the dark crumbs she spotted on the plate. There were also two glasses with traces of milk in them and a mug with signs of either tea or coffee at the bottom.

Sam found it strange that the items hadn't been rinsed through, but then, maybe the father had other things on his mind, like committing suicide. She checked the handle on the back door—it was locked. She peered out of the window and shook her head at the carnage scattered across what used to be a lawn.

And yet, there are signs that the garden had once been a pleasant place to sit and play in the past.

She decided to join her partner upstairs. He was in the main bedroom, hunting for clues in the wardrobe. Sam knew he wouldn't be as observant as she was so made her way across the room to join him.

"Found anything?"

"Everything seems okay in here. A mixture of male and female clothes, so I don't think they've split up."

"Have you had a chance to search the other rooms?" She glanced around, and her eye was drawn to a wooden box sitting on one of the bedside cabinets. Sam had an urge to investigate it further.

"Two rooms, both messy, both with single beds. I'm presuming they're the boys' bedrooms."

"I'll take a look in a moment." She ran her hand across the brass nameplate on the top of the box. "Hazel Cox. Might be the wife, or it could be either of their mothers' ashes."

"Yuck. I missed that, sorry. Kind of glad I did, though."

Sam laughed and shook her head. "It doesn't matter. We'll see what the neighbour can tell us." She left the main bedroom and dipped into the room next door. It was a lot smaller than the previous one. The single bed was made, but it wasn't straight and had several creases. Sam felt it had a man's touch rather than a woman's. Again, there was a happy picture of the family sitting on the bedside table on the other side of the room.

Unusual for teenage boys to have a family photo in their bedroom, or is it?

She moved next door and saw the exact same photo sitting on the chest of drawers in the boxroom. A single bed and a small wardrobe completed the furniture available in the bedroom.

"Anything?" Bob asked from the doorway.

"Only that I've found the same photo in here."

He frowned. "Meaning?"

"Maybe the boys' mother died, and the father printed extra copies of the photo downstairs, possibly to give the boys some comfort."

"If you say so. I can tell you now, Milly doesn't have a family photo in her bedroom."

Sam raised a pointed finger. "Which was where my mind led me. I tried to think back to my childhood. I don't recall ever having a photo of Mum and Dad in my room either, and I was really close to them."

"Interesting. I didn't either."

Sam left the room and went along the hallway to the bathroom. She hadn't noticed an en suite in the main bedroom. She turned on the light and checked how many toothbrushes were in the glass on the sink. "Three. Father and two kids," she muttered.

"You're probably right. Suddenly this place is giving me the creeps. Don't ask me why."

"I won't. Yes, I have to agree, I'm getting an uneasy feeling about this, myself. All right, let's call it quits and revisit it another time."

They returned downstairs and, from the doorway that led to the garage, Sam declared her suspicions to Des.

"Hmm... sounds logical to me. If the wife died recently

maybe the father found it impossible to cope without her. You know, raising two teenage sons can't be easy."

"A darn sight harder when grieving the loss of your partner," Sam added. "We're going to visit the neighbour. We'll reconsider the house in the future, depending on what she has to tell us."

"Let me know. I'm just waiting on my team. Apparently, they've been delayed in traffic. A likely story when we both came the same way this morning. I didn't encounter any holdups, did you?"

"Nope, drove straight through. See you later."

Sam and Bob stripped off their suits and deposited them in the black sack just outside the garage.

Sam navigated the crumbling pathway to the house next door and rang the bell. She had her warrant card in her hand and showed it to the woman in her seventies who opened the door. "Liz Chapman?"

"Yes, that's right. Do you want to come in?"

"Thanks. I'm DI Sam Cobbs, and this is my partner, DS Bob Jones."

"I'm sorry, you'll have to forgive me, I'm not thinking straight. This has come as a huge shock to me. Come through, I was just going to make a pot of tea. Can I get you one?"

"Would a coffee be too much trouble instead?" Sam asked. She wiped her feet on the mat. It was dry outside, so she didn't offer to remove her shoes but made sure Bob did the same before they followed Liz up the hallway to a large kitchen-cum-diner at the rear that, by the look of things, had been renovated recently.

"Come in. I think I have some coffee in the cupboard here. My husband and I are both tea drinkers. Correction, we were, he's no longer with me. He died during the renovations. I struggled to find a decent builder to complete the work but stumbled across Jerry after a few months. He didn't let me down."

"It's beautiful. Have you lived here long?"

"About twenty years. We took out an equity release loan against the house last year with the intention of freeing up funds to complete the kitchen. Ted suffered a massive heart attack while I was out shopping one day. I'm sorry, you don't want to hear all this. But dealing with what's happened this morning has brought it all back to me."

"There's no need for you to apologise. Why don't you take a seat and I'll make the drinks?"

"No, I'll be fine. You sit down, either at the table or the island, it's up to you. There are four stools, so no problem."

Sam pulled out one of the stools, and Bob sat next to her while Liz finished making the drinks.

"Did you come home and find your husband?" Sam asked.

"Yes, I had bags of shopping in both hands and dropped it all when I saw him lying there. He was in the doorway; he'd been ferrying some concrete in from the garden and was slumped over the wheelbarrow. He ended up facedown in it. The doctor reckoned he would have died instantly. I screamed for help, and Hazel heard my screams and came to assist me. I'm not sure what I would have done without her that day. Bless her."

"Hazel?"

"Yes, she lived next door with Steven. Lovely family, they were. She passed away six months ago. I should have noticed the signs that Steven was depressed. It never even crossed my mind that he would take his own life. Those poor kids. What will happen to them now?"

"I'm not sure. It's something that we're going to need to look into. Did they have any other family close by?"

"No, both sets of parents passed away a few years ago. Cancer killed most of them, including Hazel. Breast cancer in her case, just like her mother. Damn disease. My sister died from it a couple of years ago as well."

Having recently lost her own mother, a surge of emotion tore through Sam that she struggled to steer away. Bob nudged her leg and mouthed, asking if she was okay. She closed her eyes and nodded then sucked in a few discreet steadying breaths.

Thankfully, Liz hadn't noticed her mini meltdown. She finished preparing the drinks and joined them, choosing to sit on the stool opposite Sam. "Do you want a biscuit? I think I have some in the cupboard somewhere."

"No, don't worry, we'll be fine. Perhaps you can go over the events as they happened this morning."

Liz wrapped her hands around her mug and stared at them. "I'm usually an early riser, always have been. I got up at seven to make sure the bins were ready for when the binmen arrived. They generally show up between eight-thirty and nine-thirty, depends on the weather, I suppose. When I came back in, I fixed myself some breakfast and had a wander around the garden. I do that most mornings, if it's dry, especially at this time of the year when the plants are just coming into bud and the bulbs are at their best. I find gardening a great form of therapy now that Ted has gone."

"My grandmother used to feel the same about her garden after my grandfather passed away. I remember spending many an hour, sipping a cold drink on a deck chair while she pottered around the flowerbeds, during my frequent visits. Gran and I were very close. Sorry, this isn't about me. Please continue."

"That's lovely to hear. Children of today, well, some of them, haven't got much time for their grandparents once they reach a certain age, have they? Shame really, it was totally different in my day. Anyway, I happened to glance over the fence, it's not very high, into Steven's kitchen. The boys were eating their cereals, and it looked like he was having some toast with them. I went in not long after and jumped in the shower. I got dressed and when I pulled open the curtains, I saw Josh and Ben walk out of the gate and head off to school. It's not far, a couple of streets away."

Bob took out his notebook.

"Which school do they attend, do you know?"

"Oh yes, Pittman's High School. I used to be a teacher there, many moons ago. Ted didn't like me working, though, not after I had the kids. I didn't mind, not really, there's always plenty to do around the house, and it's not like we needed the money. Ted was on a good salary. He managed one of the local steel factories in the area. I know, you're probably wondering why we still live in a semi if he had a decent job."

"I wasn't, not in the slightest," Sam replied. "Each to their own."

"Ted invested in his future, our future, put the money away in a pension pot and paid off the mortgage on this place. That's why we decided taking some equity out of the house to pay for the renovations, it made sense at the time. We also managed to travel the world; we've been to every continent over the past twenty years. I have so many wonderful memories I can look back on and bore my children with." She chuckled and then looked guilty. "Sorry, I shouldn't be laughing at a time like this. What must you think of me?"

"It's fine. We're not here to judge you. Did you see Steven again this morning?"

"I usually see him drive off to work. I noticed his car wasn't there last night. It never occurred to me to check if everything was all right. It wasn't until I saw the dustman lingering longer than was necessary outside Steven's garage that I felt anything was wrong. I opened the front door and asked the chap what was going on. He suggested I come and hear for myself. At first, I missed what he was getting at. He told me to listen and when he stopped talking that's when I heard the car running in the garage. I don't mind telling you, fear gripped me by the throat and my heart skipped several beats. I staggered a little. The chap was called Adam. He reached out a hand to steady me and told me to call the police." She paused to take a breath and sipped at her drink.

Sam smiled reassuringly. "Take your time, there's no rush."

"Well, I came indoors, grabbed my mobile, and when I returned to see what was going on outside, three of Adam's colleagues had joined him. They were trying to figure out how to get into the garage without damaging the door. Once I got through to the emergency service operator, she told me a patrol car would be dispatched right away. The officers arrived five or six minutes later. The dustmen decided they couldn't hang around because they were behind as it was. Adam left me his phone number for the police to contact him if they need to. I have it here." She slid an envelope across the island towards Sam.

"Thanks, we'll need to get a statement from him. Can you tell me if Steven had a job?"

"Yes, he worked at the local Harper's Hardware store. That dear soul... I only wish he'd confided in me. Told me how desperate he was feeling. I might have been able to have talked him out of... you know, doing that to himself. He loved Hazel so much, was so lost when she died of cancer. He nursed her at home, right up until the end. I helped out when I could, cooked the boys' tea now and again and prepared meals for them several times a week, like casseroles, cottage pies and the like which everyone appreciated, but there was little else I could do. Steven was determined to care for his wife himself. The odd occasion he had to take one of the boys somewhere he did ask me to sit with her, but it was only for a matter of hours. It was terrible seeing her fade away like that. If God is determined to take us from this world, why on earth is He so intent on making us suffer? It's beyond me. I'm glad Ted went out the way he did, I'm hoping to go the same way... er, not exactly the same way. I meant quickly, without having to suffer for months on end like some members of my family have had to do over the years. When our time is up, end it suddenly. I think we'd all rather go that way, wouldn't we? And I don't mean taking the route Steven took today either, when I say that. Sorry, I'm going on and on here, not allowing you to get a word in."

Sam reached across and patted Liz on her hand. "Don't worry, it's probably the shock talking. What about close members of family? Did either Steven or Hazel have anyone living nearby?"

"I don't think so. Hang on, I think Hazel mentioned that Steven had a sister living somewhere on the other side of Workington, but I don't think they were that close from what I can remember."

"Any idea of her name or where we're likely to find her?"

"Gosh, now you're testing me. Dana, Delilah, Donna perhaps, it was something beginning with D. She never came to the house. Hazel just talked about her in passing one day over a cup of tea, towards the end of her life."

"Do you know where she lives or works perhaps?"

"I seem to recall Hazel saying that she was on benefits and was a lazy cow. That's not me casting aspersions on all those who receive benefits, it's not. I'm just passing on what she told me, that's all."

"It's fine. I don't suppose you know if she's married, or what her surname is."

Liz cradled her chin between her thumb and forefinger.

"Wait a minute, yes, Hazel told me that her husband had walked out on her, maybe that's why she was on benefits."

"Possibly. Do you think the boys would know where she lives?"

"I'm not sure, you'd have to ask them. I would have thought they'd know her surname or be able to give you more details than I can supply you with. If they're up to speaking with you after they find out their father has gone." She shook her head and covered her face with her hands, then the tears followed soon after.

Sam glanced at Bob whose face crinkled into a grimace. He wasn't really one for dealing with people's emotions. Sam narrowed her eyes, as if to warn him not to be so insensitive. His gaze dropped back to his notebook, and he started doodling, which annoyed Sam even more. She nudged him with her knee. He placed his pen on his pad in protest.

They waited until Liz had calmed down and was ready to continue. By that time, Sam and Bob had finished their drinks and Bob was looking decidedly pissed off, much more than normal.

Liz removed a clean tissue from the sleeve of her mint-green cardigan and blew her nose. "Please forgive me. I just can't stop thinking about what will happen to those boys now. I mean, I would step in and have them here with me, except, they're teenagers and I'm sure they will have extra emotional needs that I wouldn't be able to cope with, not at my age."

"No one would expect you to devote your life to them either. We're going to do our very best to trace Steven's sister. We'll need to get Social Services involved, maybe they'll have her details on file somewhere."

"Or maybe the school will be able to supply us with next of kin information," Bob added, shocking Sam.

"I agree. We're going to have to make tracks soon. Are

you going to be all right, Liz? Perhaps you can call a member of your family, ask them to come and sit with you?"

Liz blew her nose again and shook her head. "No, both my children lead very busy lives, I'd prefer not to be a hindrance to them."

Sam patted Liz's hand again. "I'm sure you wouldn't be."

"I'll be okay. You know what they say, a good cry cures all evil. Forgive me, I don't make a habit of breaking down in front of strangers, especially important ones such as yourselves."

"We're nothing special, just two people doing their jobs. You've been a great help to us today, and that's the best cup of coffee we've had in a long time whilst being out on the road."

Liz smiled, and the three of them hopped off their stools. She saw them to the front door and shook their hands. "I'm sorry I couldn't have been of further help to you and the boys. Will you send them my love when you break the news to them? Tell them I'm here for them if they should ever need me." Tears welled up again, and she plucked another tissue from the box on the table in the hallway. "I'm sorry, I'm sure I don't know what is wrong with me today. I'm usually the strong silent type, never one to openly show my emotions like this."

"It's the shock. That's why I think you should reconsider your decision not to get in touch with your family."

"I'll give my daughter a call. I'm sure just speaking with her will help calm me down. I wouldn't want to be a burden, especially during the week."

"I'm sure she won't see it like that. Give her a call as soon as we've gone, promise me?"

"I will. Good luck. Hope you find the information you need. I'd hate to think of those boys ending up in an orphanage, if that's where they're sent these days."

"Don't worry, I'm sure it won't come to that. Take care of yourself."

Sam smiled and resisted the temptation to give the woman the hug that she was obviously crying out for.

On the way back to the car, Bob said, "There you go again, getting too involved with a member of the public while on duty. At least you didn't hand her one of your cards."

"Shut up. Shit, you're right, I'll nip back and give her one." She pressed the key fob to unlock the car. "Get in, I'll be two ticks." She ran back to the house before he could raise an objection.

Sam knocked on the door, and Liz opened it swiftly.

"Sorry, I forgot to give you one of my cards. Ring me day or night if you either think of anything else or if you need to reach out to me for any reason."

"You're too kind, thank you, Sam. I'll leave it here, on the hallway table. I'm likely to forget where I put it if I tuck it away safely somewhere."

Sam smiled. "I'm the same. Speak soon." She tore back to the car. "Sorry for the delay."

"Whatever. Where are we going next, his work or the school?"

"I think we'll go to his workplace first. In the meantime, I'll let Social Services know what's going on so they can start the ball rolling at their end."

"Sounds a good idea. Want me to make the call?"

"Yes, why not? Do you know the school the kids go to?"

"Yep, it's the same one Milly goes to. I hope I don't run into her in the corridor, she'd die if she ever saw me on school premises."

Sam laughed. "I can relate. It happened to me once. Dad was on a job at the school in his younger days. I nearly fainted when I saw him. I was with a group of friends and chose to ignore him. Thankfully, he was concentrating on the job in hand and didn't see me."

"That was a relief." Bob dialled the number.

Sam got on the road. During the conversation, she offered him some advice, whether he wanted it or not.

He ended the call and glared at her. "You should have asked me to drive."

"Sorry, I went over the top, didn't I?"

"Yep, you definitely lack faith in my abilities, that much is evident."

"I don't. I was just trying to be helpful."

He turned and looked out of the window at the hills in the distance to their left. "More like a bloody hindrance than a help, but you're the boss."

Sam suppressed the giggle threatening to escape and bit down on her response. The trading estate where the hardware store was located was up ahead of them. She parked in a space close to the main entrance. "Are you in a better mood now?"

He removed his seatbelt and flung open the passenger door. "I'm never in a bad one."

"If you say so."

Inside the store, Sam showed her ID to the girl at the reception desk, close to the tills. "Hi, is the manager around?"

"Oh, the police. I'll have to check. He's bound to ask me what it's about; what shall I tell him?"

"That we're making enquiries into an investigation."

"I'll be right back." She left her counter and trotted up the aisle to an area near the back of the store. She returned with a man wearing a grey overall. "This is Mr White."

"Hello there. How can I help you today?"

"Hi, I'm DI Sam Cobbs, and this is my partner, DS Bob Jones. Is there somewhere private we can talk, sir?"

"Yes, my office is around the corner. You'll have to excuse

me, I'll need to wash my hands first, we had a problem with the paint colour machine."

"No worries."

He took them to his office, told them to make themselves comfortable and disappeared again.

"That's a novelty," Bob said.

"What is?"

"A boss getting his hands dirty."

She turned in her seat to face him. "What are you insinuating?"

He rolled his head back and stared at the ceiling. "Give me strength. I wasn't suggesting you don't..." He stopped talking when White entered the room.

He hung his overall on the coatrack and then sat behind his mahogany desk that was cluttered with paperwork. "Right, what can I do for you?"

"We believe you have an employee working for you called Steven Cox, is that correct?"

He exhaled a large breath. "I did. He's clearly taken umbrage to the meeting I had to have with him yesterday because he's neglected to turn up for his shift today."

"Umbrage? Can you tell us more?"

"I had to give him a third and final warning about his attitude. I did my best for him. Had a chat with him. Told him that if he showed up today with a different attitude, I would reconsider giving him his notice and would be willing to give him another chance. Well, he's obviously felt the need to throw my kindness back in my face, hasn't he? Umm... may I ask what this is all about? He's not in any kind of trouble, is he?"

A lump had appeared in Sam's throat. She tried to swallow it down and felt Bob's gaze burning into the side of her face. She coughed to clear the lump and said, "Sadly, he lost his life this morning."

Her words acted like a bullet to Mr White's chest. He crashed back against his executive chair. "He what? He's dead? I can't believe this."

"It's true."

"How? Or can't you tell me that?"

"Our initial assessment is telling us that he committed suicide, but there will be a post-mortem carried out this afternoon that will give us the true cause of death."

"Suicide. Jesus, I knew he was depressed but I never thought he would ever contemplate ending his life. I feel terrible now, having that meeting with him. It was out of necessity, though. The rest of the staff had started complaining about him. Word got back to me they were fed up carrying him. If only he had come to me with his problems... why the hell did he remain quiet about this? Shit, I'm devastated that it has come to this. I'm not sure if I'll ever be able to forgive myself."

"If he was struggling then you were entitled to pull him up about his attitude. You mentioned you thought he was depressed. Can you tell me how long that's been going on?"

"He was. I should have shown him more compassion and ignored the rest of the staff, but I fear they would have gone on strike if I hadn't stepped in and had a chat with him." He shook his head and tutted in disbelief then sat forward again. "Is there anything we can do for his boys? What will happen to them? Sorry, you asked me how long he'd been depressed, since the death of his wife. He was devoted to her and the boys. I feel guilty for not realising he needed help sooner. That guilt will remain with me for the rest of my life."

"You mustn't blame yourself. If you were unaware, then that's not down to you."

"No, I was aware that he was depressed but I never even considered to what extent. I could have helped him, made allowances for him, if only he had reached out to me and asked for help."

"That's easier said than done for some people. He must have been in a desperate state to take his life, without considering what would happen to his sons. None of us truly know how grief will affect some people."

"On the one hand I agree with you, but as manager of this store, it's my responsibility to be open enough with my staff, allowing them to turn to me for help when they're in trouble. His colleagues are going to be mortified when I tell them. I'll have to tell them, I can't possibly sit on this kind of news, they'd crucify me if word got back to them and I hadn't informed them."

"I take it he wasn't close to anyone he worked with?"

"No, I think that's right. Every time I saw him in the canteen, he was always sitting at a table alone, never really interacted with the rest of the staff. I think a couple of the men tried to get to know him, but he was a bit of a loner."

"Even before he lost his wife?" Sam asked.

"Yes, I believe she was called Hazel. She had breast cancer for a couple of years. That news rocked his world. He had a lot of time off to care for her near the end of her illness. He returned to work once the funeral was out of the way. I don't think he should have come back when he did, maybe it was too soon for him."

"People never really know if that's the case or not until they try. We have a dilemma on our hands, and I was wondering if you might be able to help us out."

He frowned and interlocked his fingers. "I can try."

"Considering what happens to the boys, we were wondering if you might have his sister's details on his personnel record."

"His sister? Ah, is she the only living relative available to take care of the lads?"

"Maybe. Steven's neighbour told us she exists but couldn't really give us any more than that, and if Steven wasn't close to any of his colleagues, then they're not likely to know anything about her, are they?"

"Sadly not. Let me see if I can pull up his file now and have a look for you. My opinion is that he probably put Hazel down as his next of kin, and between us, we forgot to update his file after she passed away."

"Maybe it's something for you to consider going forward."

"Absolutely. I totally agree with you in light of what has happened to Steven. I still can't quite believe it. I don't think I've ever known anyone who was desperate enough to take their own life before. What on earth will those kids be thinking?"

Bob's mobile rang. He excused himself and left the room. Sam presumed it was his contact at Social Services getting back to him; he would have ignored the call if it hadn't been work related.

"It's a tough situation for them to deal with. We've been in touch with Social Services; our next call will be to visit the school to let the boys know about their father."

"Can you imagine, putting yourself in their shoes, what they're going to have to contend with over the next few days, weeks, or even months? My heart goes out to them, it truly does. I'll be sure to give my daughter an extra hug when I finish work tonight. It's true what they say, none of us know what life holds for us and what lies around the corner, do we? I read the other day about a man of twenty-three who is carrying the gene for dementia. Sorry, that's going off the subject, I'm just saying... never mind."

Sam smiled. "Yes, I heard about that young man. He's turning a negative into a positive and raising awareness about the disease. I also heard that his brother took the test as well and he is also carrying the gene. They're to be admired, doing all they can for other people before the disease takes hold. Life can deal the toughest of blows when we least expect it, can't it?"

"It certainly can."

Bob came back into the room and took his seat. "Excuse me a moment, Mr White. Someone from Social Services is meeting us at the school in twenty minutes. It was the only slot they had available, so I took it."

"That's fine. We're almost done here. Mr White is just going to see what he has on file for me regarding Steven's next of kin."

"Yes, that's right. I'll do it now." He tapped a few keys on his computer, shook his head and blew out a breath. "It's as I expected, the file hasn't been updated since his wife died back in November."

"That's a shame. Not to worry. We appreciate you checking for us." Sam rose from her seat and extended her hand.

Mr White shook it. "Can you leave me one of your cards? I'll ask around the staff for you. Maybe Steven told one of them in passing. I doubt it, but it's better to be certain, isn't it?"

Sam withdrew a card from her pocket and handed it to him. "Thanks. If there's anything any of his colleagues can add it'll be a bonus at this stage. It was good to meet you, sorry it had to be under such sad circumstances."

"I'm sorry, too. Deep down he was a good man, if a little confused in the last six months."

He showed them back to the main entrance and bid them farewell.

"What did Social Services have to say for themselves?" Sam asked as she started the car. "Sorry, you're going to have to direct me to the school from here."

"No problem. Head back to the main road and take a right. They were a bit short with me, sounded to me as if they were treating the situation as an inconvenience."

"I know they're under pressure, there again, aren't we all? But do they truly think we'd be contacting them if it wasn't an emergency? They boil my piss at times."

Bob sniggered. "I'm not going there. Take a left at the top and continue on the same road for three to four minutes. It'll crop up on your left soon enough."

"Thanks, I'd literally be lost without you."

"No, you wouldn't, you have a satnav on board but most of the time you can't be arsed to use it."

Sam faced him and grinned. "I like you to feel involved." She fluttered her eyelashes at him.

"Whatever. It's a cop-out all the same. See what I did there?"

"No. Care to explain?" she said, deliberately winding him up.

"I don't think I'll bother. The woman told me her associate would meet us in the reception area."

"Good."

CHAPTER 2

Five minutes later they were standing close to reception, awaiting the person's arrival. Rather than hang around twiddling her fingers, Sam approached the receptionist and asked if it would be possible to see the head once the Social Services representative arrived.

The receptionist placed the call, and the headmistress, Mrs Lowther, agreed to see them once they were ready.

A woman in her mid-forties, wearing a black trouser suit, came hurtling through the main doors and walked towards them. She extended her hand at Bob. "I'm Georgina Marks from Social Services. Are you DS Jones?"

"I am. Pleased to meet you. This is my boss, DI Sam Cobbs."

The woman shook hands with Sam.

"Thanks for agreeing to meet us at such short notice," Sam said. "It's a difficult situation we've been thrust into. I believe the sooner we tell the boys the better. Can you tell us what will happen to them?"

"We've checked through our files and managed to obtain

the information for an aunt. I haven't made contact with her yet, thought I'd see where the land lies with the boys, first."

"That's great. What's the aunt's name?"

"Dora Barstow."

"Ah, yes, that sounds like the right one. We had a chat with the boys' neighbour this morning. She mentioned their father had a sister and her name began with a D, but she couldn't tell us much more than that."

"She is the only living relative we have on record."

"I hope she can open up her home to the boys. I dread to think what will happen to them otherwise. Are you aware they lost their mother back in November?"

"I am. It's going to be very hard for them to hear the news about their father, but between us, I'm sure we can overcome any obstacles that come our way."

"Let's hope you're right. Shall we see the head now?"

Georgina hitched up her heavy satchel on her shoulder. "Lead the way."

"Can Bob help you with your bag?" Sam asked.

"I'm fine. Once I get it in a comfortable position. I actually forget it's there most of the time."

The receptionist showed them down the length of the long corridor to the head's office. Sam almost froze when she saw two teenage boys sitting outside the head's room.

"Do you think that's them? I can't tell, my eyesight isn't good at this distance."

Bob groaned. "You need to visit Specsavers, how many more times do I have to tell you?"

"I've got glasses, I just forget to wear them sometimes."

He grumbled. "There's a surprise."

"Stop complaining and answer my bloody question."

"Yes, they look like the boys in the family photo."

"Great, see how easy that was?"

Georgina chuckled beside Sam. "I see you two have a super working relationship."

"That's debatable most days," Sam replied out of the corner of her mouth.

"I heard that," Bob said.

The receptionist knocked on the door and received the go-ahead from the head to enter. She opened the door and announced, "The police are here to see you along with a lady from Social Services."

"Okay, Tina. Thank you. Can you ask them if they'd like a drink?"

Sam shook her head. "We're fine, thanks all the same."

"I'm okay as well," Georgina replied.

They all entered the room. Mrs Lowther remained seated and gestured for them to take a seat. Three chairs had been set out ready for their arrival. Sam chose the middle seat, Bob sat on her right and Georgina on her left.

"I have to tell you this morning has been a whirlwind of emotions. Well, since you got in touch with me, Georgina, about half an hour ago. What I wasn't expecting was the police being here. I'm not sure how we should proceed with the boys. They're obviously aware that something is going on, after being summoned."

"It's a difficult one that we should be able to sort out between us," Sam said. "The last thing we want is for them to feel ambushed. Their feelings should be paramount. Saying that, I think we should all be present when the news is broken. Do you agree?"

"I agree," Georgina confirmed. "Mrs Lowther?"

Mrs Lowther clenched her fists on the desk. "It's not going to be an easy task whichever way we decide to share the news. Who do you suggest should tell them?" Her question was directed at Sam.

"I'm willing to take a back seat on this one, leave it to either of you two ladies," Sam replied.

"I don't mind breaking the news," Georgina said. "I'm used to dealing with kids who are emotionally distressed."

"Sounds good to me," Sam said.

Mrs Lowther left her chair. "I'll ask them to join us." She opened the door and quietly spoke to the boys. "Joshua and Benjamin, please come in."

Bob spotted a stack of chairs in the far corner of the room and quickly collected two of them. He placed them side by side close to Georgina.

"Thanks, Bob," Sam whispered when he returned to his seat.

Mrs Lowther closed the door behind the boys, invited them to sit, then introduced everyone before she added, "Now there's no need for you to be scared, we're all here to help you. Georgina has some news for you." She sat back, and her gaze drifted to Sam, who offered up a weak smile.

"I'm sorry to have to tell you that your father had an accident this morning and sadly died," Georgina said hesitantly.

Ben and Josh stared at each other, their expressions devoid of all emotion.

It was the older boy, Josh, who found his voice first. He asked, "We don't know what you mean. An accident? Did it happen at work? How can he die from an accident?"

Georgina glanced at Sam who saw nothing but panic in Georgina's eyes.

Sam decided to jump in and give a better explanation. "No, it happened at home. At this stage we can't give you any other information, not until a post-mortem has been carried out later this afternoon. Do you know what one of those is?"

Ben shook his head.

Josh murmured, "Yes, it's when someone cuts up a dead

body to see how a person has died. I've seen *Silent Witness* with my dad. He stopped watching it when Mum died. It got too much for him." His head dropped.

"We're sorry for your loss, boys. We're trying to get in touch with your Auntie Dora, see if she'll let you stay with her for a while," Sam leaned forward and said.

Ben put a hand in front of his mouth and leaned over to whisper in Josh's ear. Sam watched the boys' reaction to the news but couldn't really glean much from their expressions.

"Do you have her phone number or her address, boys?" Sam asked.

"No. Dad knew, but we don't have a clue. She lives on the other side of town, not sure where, though. We haven't seen her in years, she rarely visits us."

"Did she get on with your parents?" Georgina asked.

Josh shrugged. "I can't remember. I haven't seen her since I was about five or six."

"I can't remember her either," Ben added. He leaned in closer to Josh, their arms and legs touching, as if he needed his older brother to comfort him.

"Well, we're going to do our very best to find her," Georgina told them. "In the meantime, we're going to put you with a family who deals with emergencies of this nature."

"I don't understand. Why can't we stay at home, in our house? Why do we have to go somewhere else?" Josh demanded.

"Because the police are at your house, carrying out an investigation, Josh," Georgina told him. "This is the right thing to do, I promise you."

Josh's gaze flitted between Georgina and Sam and settled on Sam. "Will we be able to go back home when the police have finished?"

She smiled at the older boy. "Of course you will, but it will only be for a visit, to allow you to pack up some of your belongings to take to your aunt's house."

Josh shook his head. "That's not fair. What will happen to our home?"

It was Georgina's turn to answer. "Do you know if the house was paid for? Did your parents have a mortgage? Or was it rented?"

The boys glanced at each other, and Josh shrugged.

"I think Dad told me they had a mortgage. When Mum died and he was due to go back to work, he said he was behind on the mortgage, it's what made him go back early. He wasn't ready to handle work again, he struggled in the beginning, looking after us on his own, but we promised to help out where we could."

Sam nodded and asked, "Do you know what depression is, Josh?"

"When someone is low and finds it hard to cope with life, is that right?"

"It is. Well done. Do you know when your father's depression began?"

Ben whispered behind his hand once again, and Josh's gaze met Sam's.

"Before Mum died. Caring for her took a lot out of him. He kept telling us that he knew how Granddad felt looking after Nan before she passed away."

"Did your gran die of cancer as well?" Georgina asked.

"No, she had that dementia. We went to see her, not long before she died, and she was in a terrible state. Scared and lashing out at my granddad; she thought he was a stranger. Kept telling him to get out of her house. Granddad was really upset, and Dad had to comfort him. But it didn't make any difference. Nan died a few weeks later, and not long after that Granddad died. He had a heart attack. Dad told us that he'd died from a broken heart after losing Gran."

"That's a shame, when did this happen?"

"Two years ago. Then Mum got ill not long after. We had to prepare ourselves for her death. She clung on, put up a good fight for as long as possible, Dad told us. Ben and me, we did our best, looked after ourselves the best we could, but no one taught us how to cook or how to use the oven, and we didn't like to bother Dad. We lived on sandwiches for months. Dad lost a lot of weight because he couldn't eat. I used to take him a sandwich. He would nibble at it but nine times out of ten he'd leave most of it. It wasn't until Mum died that he started to look after us properly again, well, sort of. At least he made us hot food again, like beans on toast."

"But your neighbour, Liz, made you meals now and again, didn't she?"

Josh stared at Sam. She couldn't tell if he was challenging her or not.

His head sank once more. "Sorry, yes, I forgot about that. She's a kind lady. Can't we stay with her? At least we'll be close to home and it's nearer to school than Auntie Dora's place."

"Sadly not. Liz is getting on, and she told me to send you both her love. She's upset that she wouldn't be able to offer you a home at her age."

"We understand," Josh mumbled. "But we know her better than our aunt."

"Let's see if we can find your aunt first. When we do, all I ask is for you to give her a chance. Otherwise, you'll both need to go into care, and I can't guarantee that you won't get separated."

Ben gripped his brother's arm. "No, I don't want that. I need to stay with Josh. It's not fair to make us live separately, is it, Josh?"

"Hush now. Stay strong, Ben. He's right, why should we lose each other when we've already lost our parents?"

Georgina smiled and laid her hand on Josh's arm. "Hopefully, it won't come to that. I'm going to do my very best for you."

"Thank you," both boys mumbled.

"Good, I know you won't let Josh and Ben down," Mrs Lowther added. "They will still be allowed to come here, won't they?"

"I'm not sure, it depends on what the aunt says about getting them to school. It might not be practical, considering where she lives, but that's a bridge we'll need to cross later. What we need to do is drop by the house, pick up some clothes for both of you, just enough to see you through the next couple of days. Will that be okay, Inspector?"

"We can sort something out. My partner and I can come back to the house with you, ensure everything runs smoothly. As long as we keep out of the technicians' way, it should be fine. I'll just need to ring ahead and warn them we're on our way."

"That's a great idea, isn't it, boys?" Georgina asked.

The boys both shrugged.

"I suppose so," Josh said.

To Sam, the boys appeared to be taking everything in their stride. Yes, they seemed a little upset, but nothing too drastic at this time. Maybe the news hadn't had a chance to sink in yet.

"Let me make a call." She left the room and rang Des's mobile. "Don't shout at me, it's Sam. I'm at the school, we've just informed the two kids. Social Services are here, they're going to have to place the boys somewhere temporary for now but they're going to need to gather some of their belongings from the house. Any chance we can drop back with them in the next half an hour or so?"

"Christ, you're not asking much, are you? Do I have to remind you that this might well turn out to be a crime scene?"

"I'm well aware of that. Hey, I could have just shown up out of the blue, but I have better manners than to do that and thought I'd prewarn you first."

"Are you expecting me to be grateful?"

Sam tutted loudly, making sure he heard her. "Give me a break, Des. Will it be all right to drop by or not?"

"I'll see what I can do for you, bearing in mind that my men have only just arrived. Maybe we can section off part of the house. If we open the front door, perhaps the boys can just go straight upstairs when they get here."

"I'm sure that will be acceptable. Will thirty minutes be enough time for you to make the necessary preparations?"

"It might be."

"Des? Stop messing with me, not at a time like this."

"I'm not. I said it should be, I stand by that comment. Are we done here?"

"Yes."

He hung up on her. Sam stared at the phone and stamped her foot. *Arsehole. You can be a bloody ignorant dickhead when it suits.*

Sam rejoined the others. "Yes, that's all sorted. We should be okay to go back to the house in half an hour or so. The Scenes of Crime Officers will need to section off the house. You should only need to go upstairs, shouldn't you, boys?"

"Yes, to our bedrooms," Josh agreed. "Will we have to wear one of those paper suits I've seen the actors wear on *Silent Witness*?"

Sam smiled. "You will."

Ben nudged his brother. "Will I be able to take my games console with us?"

"I think so. Will he?"

"I don't see why not," Sam replied.

Thirty minutes later, Georgina accompanied them back to the house. Josh and Ben travelled in the car with her. Sam gathered some extra paper suits from one of the technicians without Des knowing. He had been quite possessive with them lately, and Sam had struggled to get extra supplies from him at the last couple of crime scenes.

"I'll check if everything's in place, I won't be long," she told Georgina and the boys.

She met Des in the hallway. He was busy dishing out instructions to the team. Sam stood back; she knew better than to interrupt him when he was in full flow.

"Oh, you're here already, are you? That was the quickest thirty minutes of the day."

Sam smiled. "Are you ready for us? We'll be in and out of here in no time, I promise you."

"I'm going to hold you to that. Yes, we're just doing the final tweaks now. Give the men two minutes to get organised. I want you in and out. No fuss. No extra questions from the boys while they're here. Remember, I'm doing you a favour. You know as well as I do what the procedures are about family members entering a property which we might regard as a crime scene."

"Yes, you're right, and ordinarily I wouldn't ask, you know that. This is an emergency, though."

"I'm aware of that fact, hence my willingness to be of assistance with your plight." He peered over his shoulder, and one of the technicians gave him the thumbs-up. "Bring them in. I want you in and out within ten minutes, got that?"

Sam blew out a breath. "You're a harsh man, Des Markham."

"I'm also a fair man. I'm going above and beyond here, just remember that."

"I'm not likely to forget it with you shoving it down my throat every five minutes."

He turned his back on her and slipped through an opening in the white cloth that had been hung over the garage door.

Sam went back to the car and collected the boys. Georgina asked to go with them, and Sam handed the three of them paper suits. Georgina helped Sam to fold back the hems on the legs and arms on the boys' suits. Bob remained in the car; there was no point all of them entering the house.

Sam led the way through the front door and up the stairs, casting an eye on what was going on behind her, now and then. The boys' curiosity got the better of them, and once or twice Ben stumbled as he missed the next step when his eyes were drawn to the technicians moving in the hallway below.

"Okay, let's make this quick. Do you have a sports bag or something you can fill?"

"Yes, there's a small suitcase in Dad's room as well," Josh said. "If I promise to pack it quickly, can we take that with us?"

"I don't see why not. Georgina and I will lend a hand, if you tell us what you want us to pack. Don't go throwing things in, try to put your clothes in neatly, that will give you room to take more with you."

Josh looked at her and shook his head. "We're teenagers, not infants."

Sam chuckled and ruffled his hair. "Sorry, my mistake. If you tell me where the case is in your father's room, I can fetch it for you."

"I'll get it myself." Josh ran out of the room before Sam could stop him.

Georgina accompanied Ben to his bedroom to help him pack.

Josh joined Sam a few seconds later. He had a small case in his hand. He threw it on the bed and opened it. Inside, were what appeared to be some of his mother's clothes. "Oh no, I thought it would be empty. I can't take this."

"It'll be okay. Your father probably kept a bag packed in case your mother had to be admitted to hospital at short notice. Do you want me to remove them for you?"

Teary-eyed, he shook his head. "No, I'll do it." He sat on the bed next to the case and touched the items of clothing. "I miss her so much."

Sam took a step closer and placed a hand on his shoulder. "I know how difficult this must be for you, but it's true what they say, time is a great healer."

A tear dripped onto his cheek. "How would you know?"

"Because I lost my own mother a few months ago."

"But you're older than we are. Sorry, I don't mean to be rude, but it's the truth."

"You're right, I am. I can't imagine what you and Ben must be going through, however, you need to be aware that you're not alone. There are people willing to help you."

"Like my aunt? A woman we barely know?"

"Yes, but also people in authority. I'm sure Georgina will be keeping a close eye on you both in the future. She seems a nice lady, doesn't she?"

He nodded and began removing his mother's clothes from the case. He stretched over to place them gently on his pillow at the top of the bed.

"I'll do that while you pack your sports bag."

He stood and collected his bag from the top of the double pine wardrobe. Sam continued to remove the clothes from the case and carefully added them to the pile Josh had started.

In the meantime, she kept a close eye on how Josh was doing and noticed him pause a few times. "Are you all right? Do you need a hand?"

"No. I could do with some answers."

"I'll try, what do you want to know?"

He faced her and held her gaze. "Did Dad kill himself?"

"Honestly, and I know this isn't the answer you want to hear right now, but it's all I can give you at this time. We don't know yet, not until the pathologist has had a chance to perform the post-mortem."

"What does your gut tell you?"

Sam sat on the end of the bed and nodded. "Yes, I believe your father took his own life." She patted the quilt beside her, inviting him to join her.

"I thought so. He hasn't been the same, not since Mum died. It was hard for us, too, you know."

"I'm sure it must have been hard on all of you. Sometimes adults find the pressure of everyday life extremely difficult to handle. Do you know if he tried to get any counselling? I take it you understand what that means?"

He rolled his eyes at her. "Of course I do. No, he didn't. He tried to show us how okay he was most days, I think more for Ben's sake than mine. I used to stay up later with him. Now and again, I would catch him sitting at the table in the kitchen with his head in his hands. When I asked him what was wrong, he told me he had a headache he couldn't shift. I knew he was lying. I did try to get him to open up to me, but it was as though he was determined to shield us from the truth."

"Adults always do their best to protect their children. Sometimes that backfires on them."

"He didn't have to kill himself, all he needed to do was reach out to someone for help."

"You have a wise head on your shoulders, Josh. How old are you?"

"Fifteen. I know the difference between right and wrong, at least I think I do in most cases. It's Ben I feel sorry for, he's young for his age and has suffered so much. Mum was really bad at the end. Again, Dad prevented us from seeing her most days, but now and then Ben and I would sneak in to sit with her while Dad made a sandwich or a drink. It was usually my idea. I thought Ben should know what Mum was going through, it's the best way, to be honest and open with someone, isn't it?"

"Yes, sometimes shielding loved ones from the truth at such a sad time can be wrong on so many levels. You did the right thing." Sam smiled. "I know in my heart you're brave enough to get through this, Josh. I'm going to make sure I leave you one of my cards, you can ring me at any time, day or night, if ever you feel the need to chat with someone who is aware of what you're going through."

Tears emerged in his sad brown eyes. "Thank you, that means a lot to me. You seem a really nice lady. I'm sorry about your mum. Was she ill?"

"Only for a short while, but at least I got the chance to say goodbye to her."

"I'm glad. Dad allowed us to sit with Mum on the final day. Ben found it a struggle to be in the same room with her. It was hard for him to listen to the death rattle. I admit it was difficult for me, too, but I felt it was important for us to be there, if only to support Dad. Why did he have to kill himself? We need him, now more than ever, and he took the coward's way out. That is what they say when someone ends their life, isn't it?"

"It is, not that I've ever agreed with that notion. I feel for you, Josh, but you seem a very sensible lad to me. You'll get through this."

"I will. I'm determined to, for Ben's sake. He's the one who is going to struggle. Mum's death knocked him for six. I don't think Dad going has really hit him."

"I have such admiration for you, Josh, you're an amazing young man. Don't ever change."

He smiled, and his cheeks tinged with colour. "I have Ben to look after, we'll get through this together."

"I have no doubt about that. Right, we'd better get a wriggle on, otherwise the nasty pathologist will have my guts for garters, literally."

"Mum used to say that all the time, but she could never tell me where the saying came from."

Sam grimaced. "I'm not sure I know the true answer to that one, either." She finished removing the rest of his mother's clothes and then held the sports bag open for him so he could quickly pack the underwear and T-shirts he had in his hand.

"I think I should pack some towels, one for each of us."

"That's a great idea. I'll get them. Will they be in the airing cupboard?"

"Yes, next to the bathroom."

Sam left his bedroom and passed Ben's room on the way. She popped in to see how things were going and found Georgina sitting on the bed next to Ben. She had her arm around him. The poor lad was sobbing his heart out.

Sam crept up beside them and then knelt on the floor in front of Ben. She put her hand over his. "Hey, it's okay to be upset. No one is going to think badly of you."

"I don't know what we're… going… to do… now that Mum and Dad are both gone. I don't think I'll ever be able to smile again, ever."

"Nonsense, of course you will. You have Josh. He's promised me he's going to take care of you. Is he the type of person to break a promise?"

Ben sniffled and wiped his nose on the cuff of his jumper. Sam closed her eyes and cringed.

"No, he never lets me down. But… it shouldn't be down to him… to look after me, should it?"

Sam opened her eyes again. "You're right, that's why we're going to try our best to find your aunt."

"I've had a call from one of my colleagues, they think they've found her. I have an address to try. I'd much rather take the boys there than put them with a foster family."

"That's great news, isn't it, Ben?"

The boy hitched up a shoulder. "I dunno."

"What's going on? Have you upset him?" Josh shouted from the doorway. He ran towards them.

Sam quickly got to her feet. "He's fine. He's just a little upset. Ben's just wondering what's going to happen to you both in the future."

Josh took his brother's hand and pulled him into a hug. "It'll be all right, bro. I'm never going to let you down."

Ben sobbed and slipped his arms around his brother's waist.

"How's it going up there?" Des shouted up the stairs.

"Damn. Sorry to break this up, boys, I have a big bad pathologist breathing down my neck. He gave us ten minutes to gather all your stuff. I think our time is up. Are you ready, Ben?"

He sniffled again. "Yes, I think so. No, wait, I need to pack a few games and my console."

"Don't worry, Georgina will help you. I'll fetch the towels and bring them in to you, Josh. Are you nearly packed now?"

"Yes. I came in to see if Ben wants to take any jumpers with him. There's room in the case for a couple."

"Yes, I'll get them." Ben tore around the room collecting the items he needed.

Sam went to the top of the stairs to speak with Des. "Two minutes maximum. Sorry, the boys got a bit upset."

"I don't want or need your excuses, we had a deal."

Sam's blood boiled. *Does the man have no compassion left in him?* "Give me a break, Des. I'm doing my best in exceptionally challenging circumstances."

He grunted and turned on his heel without saying another word.

Sam raised her eyes to the flaking ceiling and slapped her arms against her thighs. *Men! What is bloody wrong with them?* Then she opened the airing cupboard and removed two blue bath sheets. She took them back to Josh and asked, "What about your toiletries, have you collected those yet?"

"Not yet. I'm done here now." He ran past her and headed towards the bathroom. He emerged with a toiletry bag, loaded with necessities, a few minutes later.

With everything packed, Sam closed the lid of the suitcase and locked it. Josh attempted to carry the case and his sports bag, but Sam relieved him of it.

"I'll take it. Let's hope Ben has found all he needs and is ready to go."

"He'll be fine."

Ben and Georgina appeared on the landing and led the way down the stairs. Bob saw them and got out of the car to assist them. He put the bags in the boot of Georgina's car. Georgina settled the boys in the back of her car and read a text message on her phone.

"I've got it. I can take it from here, if you like?"

Sam handed Georgina a card. "Can you let me know how they get on, later?"

"I sure will. Thanks for all your help today. You missed your vocation, you were brilliant with the kids in there. I can tell they really trust you."

"Makes a change for a copper to have a good impact on children."

"You're telling me. Thanks again. I'm sure it won't take them long to get settled."

Georgina got in her car, and the two boys waved until Sam became a spot in the distance. She turned back to the house with a tear in her eye.

"Soppy mare. There you go again…"

Sam raised a hand, cutting Bob off. "It's called having empathy for those in need. You want to try it sometime. I'm going to have a quick chat with Des before we leave."

"You'll be chancing your luck, the mood he's been in today."

"Nevertheless, I'm going to risk it. You can stay in the car, rather than waste another suit."

"You're the boss."

Sam ignored his sarcasm and tentatively stepped back inside the house. "Des, are you free?"

The door to the lounge opened. "Have they gone?"

"The boys? Yes. Why? What have you found?"

She followed him into the room. He held up a plastic evidence bag and gave it to her.

Sam frowned and read the letter. Stunned, she shook her head. Fresh tears filled her eyes. She coughed to clear the melon-sized lump wedged in her throat. "Where did you find it?"

"On the sofa, behind one of the cushions."

"My God, it's heartbreaking. He's poured his heart out to the boys. It states how much he felt he'd let them down. Tells them how much he loves them but states it's not enough for them. Then he says how much he misses his wife and how desperate he is to be with her."

"I know, I've read it." Des sighed and ran a hand through his short hair.

Sam had no doubt in her mind how much the note had chipped away at his hardened heart. "Are you all right?"

"Honestly? I'm not sure. I don't think I've ever come across anything as devastating as this before, during my career. I've always felt performing a post-mortem gave the victim their chance to tell me what happened to end their life, but now, I have to go into the PM this afternoon, knowing exactly what Steven Cox was thinking when he attached the pipe, started the car and intentionally took his own life." He swallowed and shook his head.

"I'm sorry. I'm not sure what else to say. Do you think we should show it to the boys?"

"No, at least, not yet. They're still trying to process the loss of their father. To confront them with how much his raw emotions contributed to his death... well, it's up to you, but I wouldn't."

"I agree. Like I said, it's heartbreaking. The man's desperation led to drastic measures that no one can comprehend."

"Absolutely. God, I hate suicide cases, they eat away at my soul. Maybe the people around him missed the signs, his cries for help."

"Or maybe he simply covered his depression well, hid it long enough that those around him didn't notice in the end."

"I fear we could stand here and speculate about it all day long, but I have work to do, as I'm sure you do. Although, now that we have agreed this is a suicide, it's an open-and-shut case for you, isn't it?"

"I suppose it is, except it feels anything but right now. When you get back to the lab, can you ask one of the technicians to run a copy of the letter off and email it to me? I'd still like to keep it on record."

"I'll do that. Try not to dwell on this too much, Sam." Des rubbed her arm.

She wondered if his kind words were to do with the fact

that she'd lost her own husband to suicide. Now, that was a time of her past she definitely had no intention of revisiting. "I'll try not to. Thanks, Des. No doubt we'll see each other soon."

"That, my dear lady, I would say is a forgone conclusion."

"What about the PM? I take it my presence isn't needed this time around?"

"Correct."

"Fair enough." Sam left the house and drove back to the station. Her subdued mood didn't go unnoticed by her partner.

"Please don't tell me you're getting emotionally involved in this one?"

"I'm not. I'm simply contemplating what drives a father to take his own life when he has two teenage boys already suffering the loss of one parent and who are likely crying out for his love."

"Shit happens. Who knows how anyone is going to react when their partner dies, whether they have kids or not? By the sounds of it, losing his wife took a hell of a lot out of him."

"And the boys. I forgot to tell you, our attendance is no longer required for the PM this afternoon."

"So, Des has decided it's a suicide after all, has he?"

"When I went back to the house, he'd discovered a suicide note Steven had written for his kids."

"Shit. Glad they weren't the ones who found it. What did it say?"

"Quite a lot. I've asked Des to send me a copy via email, I should get that this afternoon. You can read it for yourself when it comes through."

"Sounds ominous."

"I think it explains a lot of the turmoil Steven must have been experiencing, leading up to him taking his own life. My heart genuinely goes out to those kids, losing both of their parents within six months of each other."

"Would counselling help them? Maybe it would be advantageous for them to see someone now, while they're still young, rather than allowing their emotions and any likely thoughts of despair take hold. We wouldn't want them ending up like their father, would we?"

"I might have a word with Rhys when I get home."

"Now that's the smartest thing you've said all day."

"Up yours, partner."

CHAPTER 3

Over the next couple of days, Sam found it impossible not to think about the two boys. Even at home, her evenings had been consumed with Rhys going over what to do next for them. He had promised her that he would have a word with one of his associates who dealt with children as he would be out of his comfort zone offering any advice for them.

Georgina was true to her word and had called Sam after she had settled the boys in at their aunt's house. Georgina seemed happy enough to leave the boys with the surprised aunt who had welcomed them with open arms.

If the boys were happy, then why did she have a really bad feeling in the pit of her stomach all the time?

Bob arrived on the Wednesday and knocked on the door to her office. "You're early, again. Anything wrong?"

"You know me, always eager to begin my day and get stuck into the mindless chore of going through my emails and internal post. It's the highlight of my day."

"She said through gritted teeth. Do you want a top-up?" He pointed at her cup.

"I thought you'd never ask. If it's not too much trouble for you, I'd love one, thanks."

He left the door ajar and returned carrying two mugs a few minutes later. She groaned inwardly, aware of the lecture brewing.

"Have you got time for a chat?"

She frowned and gestured at the seat in front of her. Maybe she was guilty of misinterpreting his intentions. "What's up?"

He sank into the chair and held his mug in his lap. "I'm after some advice really."

Sam picked up her mug and sat back, giving him her full attention. "The great Bob Jones coming to me for advice. I must make a note of it in my diary."

He went to stand.

"Sit down. You need to learn how to take a joke now and again, matey."

"Sorry, I was being serious, and here you are, treating me like an idiot."

"Whoa, that's a bit OTT. Go on, I'm all ears. Pray tell, what's on your mind?"

He glanced down at his mug and ran a finger around the rim.

"Bob? Is everything all right at home? Is Abigail okay? Is something wrong with Milly? Talk to me."

He gulped and then took a sip of his drink which he swilled around in his mouth, she presumed because it was dry.

"You're worrying me now. Spit it out, and I'm not talking about your drink!"

He swallowed his coffee and smiled. "You know me so well, or think you do."

"I have my moments. I wish I knew you well enough to work out what's going on with you at the moment."

He took another sip from his mug and then sighed. "I think Milly is being bullied at school."

Sam bolted upright, almost spilling her drink in the process. "Damn. What? What makes you think that?"

"She's changed. Her attitude towards Abigail and me, it's snarky, and she's what I would call unresponsive to us. If you get my drift?"

"I think so. Silly question, but have either of you sat down with her and asked her outright what's wrong?"

"We've tried, believe me. She just clams up. She told Abigail last night that she's dealing with it. Whatever that's supposed to mean."

"Crap! Well, my obvious answer is that she's a teenager who is going through puberty. You need to think back to when you were her age. I bet you were anything but a saint with your parents."

"Granted, I'll give you that one. But her attitude towards us has changed overnight. My attitude towards my parents began when I was thirteen and lasted until I was thirty-odd." He smiled, but it didn't last long. "No, seriously, I think if it had to do with puberty, she would have shown signs of it before now."

"What is she, fourteen or fifteen?"

"Fifteen, just, her birthday was last month."

"Okay. I'm going to ask you another question, and you have to promise you're not going to bite my head off."

"I can't do that until I hear what the question is."

"Does she have a boyfriend?"

"Not as far as I know. God forbid, that thought never even crossed my mind. If she has, then both Abigail and I have been purposely left in the dark."

"Here's another thought for you. Could she be pregnant?"

He slammed his mug on the desk, spilling some of the

contents. "What are you insinuating? That Milly sleeps around?"

"Did I say that?" she screeched. "Stop overreacting to everything I say. I'm trying to help you get to the bottom of your problem. You need to ask yourself, first, has she got a boyfriend you don't know about, and second, if they might be having sex yet. Raging hormones at fifteen is a common issue some, I'm not saying all, parents have to deal with. Again, you need to cast your mind back to when you were a fifteen-year-old lad and how often you tried getting into a girl's knickers."

He got to his feet.

"Sit down," she ordered and pointed at the chair.

"I came here for advice because I think she's being bullied, and here you are, talking about boys getting into her effing knickers. If my blood wasn't boiling before it bloody well is now, thanks to the image you've instilled in my mind."

"I'm sorry. What I'm trying to do is cover all the bases."

"As a father, correction, as a parent, I don't even want to believe that my daughter is having underage sex."

"But it's possible. That's something you're going to need to get your head around, Bob."

He ran his hand around his face and across the stubble on his chin. "No, I'm not going there. I think, in my heart, that this is about her being bullied. My question to you is, how do I get her to open up to us?"

She slapped a hand over her chest. "What am I, the bloody oracle? Do I have kids? No. So why put me on the spot?"

"Because you have a way with kids. You proved that the other day with Ben and Josh."

"I did nothing of the sort. I treated them like young adults, not as emotional teenagers. All I did was show them a teeny-weeny bit of compassion, and suddenly I'm a teenager whisperer or something along those lines, when nothing could be further from the truth."

"All right, maybe you were the wrong person to see about this. Forget I said anything."

"I will not. I offered my advice, it's up to you whether you take it on board or not. What about ringing Mrs Lowther and running it past her? She seemed nice enough when we met her the other day, didn't she? Have you ever had an issue with her before?"

"No. Never. I'll see if Abigail will do it."

"Coward."

"Charming. Not at all, my thinking is that two women will probably get on better than a headmistress speaking to a father who is likely to blow his top if the conversation doesn't go his way."

"Now that I can understand. You're not the most patient man to have ever walked the planet, are you?"

"Will you stop slating me at every opportunity that comes your way?"

Sam laughed. "Get a life. When have I ever done that to you and meant it?"

"I'll get back to you on that one, later."

"See, you can't think of an occasion." Sam's phone rang. "Saved by the bell. Excuse me a moment."

Bob left the room. "Thanks for the advice," he muttered and closed the door behind him.

"Hello, DI Sam Cobbs, how may I help?"

"Hello, Sam. It's Georgina Harrison. Is it convenient to have a chat with you?"

"Hi, Georgina, of course. What's on your mind?"

"I didn't know whether I should call you or not. It's about Ben and Josh Cox."

There was something in Georgina's tone that didn't sit well with Sam. She braced herself for what was about to come, fearing the worst. "What about them? Have they not settled at their aunt's?"

"Yes, all went well there. Umm... last night, just before I finished work for the day, I received a call from the hospital to say that Ben had been admitted."

"What? Why? No, don't tell me he tried to kill...? Sorry, I'm not able to finish my sentence."

"No, nothing like that. He was beaten up by a group of boys on his way home from school."

"Shit! Is he all right?"

"Not really. He has a couple of broken ribs, a broken arm and broken nose, plus he's suffering from concussion because the mongrels whacked him over the head with a metal bar."

"Oh my days, how bloody awful. What about Josh? Was he with his brother at the time?"

"No, he stayed behind to see one of the teachers. He asked Ben to wait for him at the school gates, but Ben decided he knew best and began walking home. This was the outcome. As you can imagine, Josh was so upset when I arrived at the hospital."

"Crap, I can hear it in your voice. I'm guessing he was the one who found Ben, am I right?"

"You are. What is wrong with people? Haven't those poor boys been through enough already, without having to contend with this kind of shit?"

"I agree. I'll drop by and see Ben when I can, hopefully this morning. Will he be up to receiving visitors?"

"I'm sure the hospital will make an exception for you and that the boys would love to see you. They wouldn't stop talking about you in the car. Ben even asked if there was a chance you would adopt them."

"Bless them. If only that were possible. I think my fiancé would have something to say about that, though."

"I bet. I'm going to try and make as many visits as possible over the coming days, while he's still there. If only to keep his spirits up. You know what it's like when you're stuck in hospital, left to your own devices. The boredom takes hold fast, and who knows where that could lead to in Ben's case?"

"How true. Okay, let me see what I can find out about the assault at this end. Do you want to give me your mobile number and I'll get back to you with any news?"

Georgina gave her the number, and Sam wrote it down on a scrap piece of paper.

"One last question: did Ben say if he recognised the boys who attacked him?"

"He wouldn't tell me, he just shrugged. My opinion would be that he knew who they were but is too scared to say anything."

"Yeah, I think you're probably right. Leave it with me and I'll get back to you soon."

Sam ended the call and finished off her cup of coffee while the news Georgina had delivered had the chance to sink in.

Once she'd digested the information properly, she got on the phone to the desk sergeant, Nick Travis. "Hi, Nick, it's DI Sam Cobbs, are you free to talk?"

"I am. I can take the call out the back if you'd rather. I have Kathy here on duty with me."

"Unless you fancy coming up here for a quick coffee with me?"

"Now there's an offer I can't refuse. I'll be with you in two minutes."

"Good man."

Sam stretched her arms above her head to release the tension that had suddenly appeared in her shoulders and left the office. Bob was staring at his computer screen. She crossed the room and perched her backside on the desk beside him. "How's it going?"

"What?"

"Okay, what I meant to say is, how are you doing?"

"I'm fine," he replied stiffly. "What's wrong with your face?" he asked quietly so the rest of the team didn't hear him.

"I've just received a call from Georgina."

"And? And, are the boys all right?"

"No, Ben is in hospital."

"How? Why? Jesus, this is bad news."

"Isn't it. He was assaulted by a gang of thugs. He's got several broken bones and concussion. Nick's on his way up to see me now. I'm going to pump him for information, see what he can tell me about the assault, then I intend visiting Ben in hospital. It's not like we're inundated with work at the moment, is it?"

"You don't want to be shouting about that, you know how keen the DCI's ears are. Heck, as if that poor kid hasn't been through enough already."

"That's what I said."

"This gang, what do we know about them?"

"Georgina couldn't get anything out of Ben. My suspicious mind is telling me that he was probably confronted by bullies from the same school."

Bob's eyes widened. "The same school as Milly. Fuck! What if my suspicion is correct?"

Sam raised a hand. "Hold it right there, mister. That's a bit far off the mark, even for you. There's a difference between bullying a teenage girl and a group of lads pounding the shit out of a teenage boy."

"Is there? Who says they limit their bullying to just boys?"

Sam tilted her head from one side to the other. "Hmm…

okay, that's a fair point. Let's not make any further assumptions until Nick fills us in on the facts."

With that, Nick entered the incident room, and Sam walked over to the drinks area to make them both a coffee.

"Er, I'll have another cup if there's one going spare," Bob shouted.

"Anybody else want one while I'm at it?"

She ended up making coffee for the whole team, and Claire offered to distribute them for her. Chore completed, she turned to Nick. "Shall we take this into my office?"

He nodded and followed her in.

From the doorway, she called over her shoulder, "Bob, do you want to join us?"

He shot out of his seat and brought his coffee with him. "I'll grab another chair."

Sam sat behind her desk. "Take a seat, Nick."

The sergeant didn't look awkward, having stepped out of his usual environment to speak with her.

Bob clattered the chair legs against the woodwork and slammed the door shut behind him. "Sorry."

"Right, what can you tell us about the attack, Nick?"

"We received a call at around five-fifteen from a distraught young man who turned out to be the victim's brother."

"We know the boys. Their father was the man who committed suicide on Monday."

"I should have realised when I took note of the surname. Not good. They've been to hell and back this week."

"Haven't they just? Have any witnesses come forward?"

"No one yet. Although, when I searched the system for any similar attacks in the area recently, a couple were highlighted."

Sam tilted her head. "Can you tell me more? I'll bring them up on the system later."

"Other victims, both teenagers, twelve and fourteen, when questioned refused to say who their attackers were. Fortunately, a witness saw the last attack. They caught some of it on their mobile phone, but when the footage was viewed, it was taken from too far away to have been considered of much use."

"We rarely get a break with incidents like this, do we?" Bob admitted. "The gangs are more intelligent than most people give them credit for."

"You're not wrong," Sam said. "However, they can't be allowed to get away with terrorising this community. Did the witness say how many there were? Could they give any type of description for the youths?"

Nick sighed and shifted in his seat. "Not really, his information was a bit vague."

"Because of possible repercussions?"

"Your guess is as good as mine."

"I'm presuming the three attacks happened out of sight of any CCTV cameras?"

"Unfortunately," Nick replied.

"Intentional then," Bob chipped in.

Sam cradled her chin between her thumb and finger. "Sounds as though they were organised attacks, doesn't it? Maybe the victims were followed for a few days and then ambushed by the thugs in a location where there weren't likely to be any witnesses. How badly hurt were the other two victims?"

"The first boy got off lightly compared to the second, who ended up in hospital like the lad last night."

"So, the crimes are getting worse, leaving us scratching our heads and wondering where it will end. Are these youths schoolkids? Bullies from this one particular school, targeting fellow pupils? It's mind-blowing to even contemplate this is going on and no one has been arrested for the crimes. So what's the answer? Patrol cars continuously circulating the area?"

"I think it will come to that eventually," Bob said. "Maybe we should think about putting undercover cops in that particular area. What time were the attacks, Nick?"

"Similar sort of time, just after school has kicked out. The witness stated that a couple of the youths had bikes, but he couldn't identify what type they were."

"What about patrolling the area with unmarked police cars, do you think that would help?" Sam asked.

"Possibly. It's got to be worth a try."

"Right, keep me informed about what you decide. We're going to visit Ben in hospital now. The boy appeared to warm to me the other day. I'll see if I can worm any more information out of him. Maybe he'll have confided in his brother. No doubt he'll be at the hospital later. We can drop back and see him after school kicks out, if we have to."

"Or visit the school to see him," Bob said.

"We'll see how it goes with Ben, then decide."

Nick finished his drink and left the room.

Sam slammed her fist on the desk. "What an absolute nightmare this is."

"I wonder why the aunt didn't call you," Bob said.

"The same question has been running through my mind during the last few minutes. I haven't got a contact number for her so I can't chase it up. I need to rectify that, once we've visited Ben. Hopefully, she'll be at the hospital."

"And if she's not?"

"We'll deal with that later; I'll ask Georgina for the number. For now, I want to get the team working on this in our absence. Liam can get cracking on the CCTV angle with Oliver, and the others can source the information from the previous attacks, which will allow us to form a better picture of what we're actually dealing with here."

"I think we pretty much know all we need to know on that front. There's a group of thugs picking off victims from a certain school. The question we need to turn our attention to is, why? Is this purely down to bullying, or is there something far more sinister at play here?"

"We'll know soon enough. Let's get things rolling. Be ready to shoot off in ten minutes."

During the journey to Whitehaven hospital, around twenty minutes up the road, Sam's stomach managed to tie itself into painful, large knots. Her breathing had become heavier without her even realising it.

"Are you all right? Because from where I'm sitting, it seems to me as though you're having some kind of panic attack."

"What? Don't be so absurd. I'm not denying this case is getting under my skin but not in a bad way."

"Eh? Is there any other way? You know, if it's getting under your skin, isn't that supposed to mean something is bad?"

"Smart arse, stop dissecting everything I say."

"I wasn't aware that I was."

"Anyway, there's one thing about this all emerging today."

He faced her and frowned. "And that is?"

"That it succeeded in taking your mind off your own problems, or should I say Milly's problem?"

"Hardly. It's still there, lingering like a foul smell. All this has done is highlight, to me anyway, that the school has an issue with bullying."

Sam parked the car in the nearest space and turned off the engine. "You can't go jumping in feetfirst, not until we're aware of all the facts. For a start, the attacks happened off school premises. Which is going to prevent us from going to the head and reporting that she has a problem at her school."

He thumped his thigh with his hand. "Why do you always have to be right?"

She smiled. "Slowly, slowly, catchy monkey, isn't that the old saying?"

"You tell me, I've never heard of it before. Which means?"

"In other words, we need to take our time with this investigation, put it together piece by piece without either pissing Mrs Lowther off or stepping on her toes."

Bob removed his seatbelt and flung open the car door. "And how do you propose we do that? Bearing in mind the evidence we've got at our disposal so far is pointing at the school having a severe issue?"

"Let me think about that. All you need to do is follow my lead on this one."

He mumbled something she didn't quite hear and got out of the car.

Over the roof, she asked, "Are you going to have the courage of your convictions and tell me what you said?"

"My usual response to situations like this, whatever."

She shook her head and glared at him. "I mean it, Bob, I can see how emotionally taut you are right now. You're going to need to rein it in until something substantial comes our way."

"Hey, it's not me who was getting all wound up in the car. Maybe this is a case of practice what you preach. Either way, I'm willing to take a step back and follow your lead. There's nothing new there, it's what I do best."

Sam smiled. "Come on, let's see how Ben is and what we can do for the lad."

The receptionist told them which ward Ben was on. The hospital shop was on the same level, and Sam stopped off to buy Ben a small box of chocolates.

"Big softie," Bob chastised her with a quirky smile.

"He deserves to be spoilt after what he's had to contend with this week."

The nurse behind the desk on the ward welcomed them. After Sam told them why they were there, she accepted their reason but asked them to be quiet during their visit, so they didn't disturb the other patients on the ward, some of whom were very poorly.

"You have our word. How's he doing?" Sam asked.

"He's very tearful and has become withdrawn since his admittance. He's due to have another CT scan later. The consultant is keen to keep an eye on the injury he sustained to his head. His brother is in there with him."

Sam and Bob glanced at each other. "Oh, I see. I presumed he would have been at school."

"He told me the head had allowed him a few hours off to be with his brother. He showed up the second the social worker left, at around nine-thirty this morning, and has been here ever since."

"I hope we don't spook him. How's Josh holding up?"

"He seems distraught and very protective of his brother. Not surprising, given the kids' backgrounds. We're all aware of what they've been through lately."

"It's been harrowing for them. This was definitely something they could have done without."

She smiled and left her desk. "Let me take you to them."

She showed them down the length of the ward to a screened-off bed at the bottom. "Hello, boys, it's only me. I've got someone here to see you, there's no need to be nervous or upset."

"Who is it?" Josh asked.

The nurse stepped aside. At first Josh smiled, as if happy to see them, but realisation quickly dawned on him, and he seemed nervous.

"Hello, Josh, Ben. Thank you, Nurse, we'll be fine and we promise to keep the noise down."

"Let me fetch you an extra chair."

"Tell me where it is and I'll get it," Bob offered.

Sam entered the curtained-off area and placed her hand on Josh's shoulder. "You're not in any trouble for skipping school. That is what you've done, isn't it?"

Josh chewed on his bottom lip and nodded. "Ben needs me. No one understands the relationship we have. He's more than a brother to me, he's my best friend. They tried to tell me to keep away, but I knew I had to be here. He's confused enough as it is, you know, after what happened to Dad…" He fell silent and stared at his brother.

Sam's heart jolted the second she laid eyes on Ben. His face was black and blue, he had a bandage wrapped around his head, two black eyes from the broken nose the thugs had given him and a plaster on his right forearm. "Oh, Ben, you have been in the wars, haven't you? Hopefully these will cheer you up." She handed him the chocolates.

The boy's head lazily turned towards her. "Thank you," he mumbled.

She could tell he was drowsy from the medication. "Have they told you how long you're going to be in hospital?"

"No. They won't tell me anything because I'm not an adult," Josh replied.

"What about your aunt? Where's she, Josh?"

The older boy hitched up a shoulder, and his gaze drifted to his brother. "Who knows?"

Sam got the impression that Josh wasn't too enamoured with his aunt.

"Is she at work? Couldn't she get time off?"

"She doesn't work. She's sat at home on her backside all day."

Bob joined them, and he and Sam sat on the opposite side

of the bed to Josh. Sam watched his expression cloud over and saw what appeared to be rage emerge. His fists clenched and unclenched on the bed beside his brother.

"Are you happy there?" Sam asked, unsure what else to say.

His eyes flickered shut, and his mouth twisted. "It's okay," Josh replied.

Sam felt his response was somewhat reluctant. She was at a loss to know how to proceed. After a few seconds' pause, she asked quietly, "Can you tell us what happened to you, Ben?"

"He can't. You can see he's not up to talking," Josh bit back. "I'm sorry, I didn't mean to snap at you. It's been a traumatic couple of days, and my brother just needs to get some rest. He's in no fit state to answer any questions about the attack."

"I understand. I apologise for pushing Ben, but the more he can tell us the quicker we can begin the investigation and bring whoever is guilty of hurting him to justice."

"You won't be able to because he was pounced on from behind, he didn't see who hurt him."

"Is that what he told you, Josh?"

"Yes."

"Did you witness any of the attack? Or see the people responsible?"

"No. When I got there, he was writhing around in pain on the ground. There was a couple walking their dog; I begged them to call the police. I couldn't charge my phone because I left the charger at the house. I need to go back there and pick it up."

"We can arrange that. Do you know where it is?"

"In the kitchen, I think. I'm not sure. I can't think straight. I'm too worried about Ben. Look at him, does he seem okay to you? I thought he'd be wide awake and able to talk to me by now."

"He's probably on extra-strong painkillers. I'm sure the staff are doing their best for him, Josh. He's suffering from a lot of bad injuries, and they're going to take time to heal. The more rest he gets in the early days, the quicker he's going to mend."

Tears welled up in Josh's tired eyes. "I know all that. I'm not stupid."

"I'm sorry, I know you're not. In fact, you're far from it. Have you eaten this morning? When was the last time you had something to drink?"

"I can't remember. I came straight here, pleaded with them to let me sit with him. I know how scared Ben will be with all this going on around him."

"The concussion will be taking its toll on him. Maybe we should talk elsewhere, give him a chance to catch up on some sleep, what do you reckon?"

Josh adamantly shook his head. "No, I can't leave him. Please don't force me to do that," he pleaded, his voice rising.

Sam placed a finger to her lips. "You need to keep your voice down or they'll kick us out."

"Sorry. He needs me to be with him. He's so scared most of the time. If only he hadn't wandered off like that. I told him to wait by the school gates for me, but his impatience got the better of him, and this is the result. Those bastards need to pay for what they did to him."

"Do you have any idea who did this? Could it be someone from school?"

He shrugged.

"Has anyone threatened either you or Ben before?"

His gaze fell on his brother's face, and he shook his head. "No."

The way he'd said it, avoiding eye contact with her, made

Sam question the validity of his response. Experience told her when to back off and when to prod an interviewee for a better answer. She decided to back off and sat there for a moment or two, taking in the touching scene that was going on between the two brothers.

"Are you intending to stay here all day, Josh?"

"That's the plan. I know I'll get into trouble for it with the head, but Ben needs me to be with him. When the medication wears off, he's going to freak out. I won't allow that to happen. Can you help me out, have a word with the school for me? Mrs Lowther? She'll understand more if it comes from a responsible adult like yourself."

"Leave it with me. I can't see any harm in you wagging school for the day, but I think you should go back tomorrow. I need to assure you that Ben is in the safest hands possible here, the staff will take good care of him. Can't your aunt do her share? Come and sit with him for a couple of hours so you don't miss out on too much of your schoolwork?"

"You can ask her, if you see her. When I left the house this morning she was still in bed. I told her I was coming to see Ben…" His voice drifted off again.

"And what was her response?"

"I didn't really get one."

"Did she indicate if she was going to be coming in later?"

"No."

Sam noticed the slight dip in Josh's head and shoulders. "Is everything all right at home?"

He shrugged. "It's early days. I suppose we're still getting to know each other."

"But you think she should be here with Ben?"

Josh looked her in the eye. "Don't you?"

"Do you have her number? I'll give her a call, see what she has to say for herself."

"No, my phone is dead."

"Ah yes, okay. I'll contact Social Services and get the number from them."

"No, don't do that. I don't want to get into trouble."

Sam raised her hand. "All right. I won't push the issue for now. We'll have to revisit it again later, though. Your aunt should be here with you, she's classed as your guardian now. That gives her a legal responsibility."

Josh puffed out his cheeks. "I don't know and I don't care. All I'm concerned about is Ben and how long it's going to take him to get better."

"Well, I'm no expert, but given the injuries he's sustained, I'm going to put my neck on the block and say I think it's going to be a couple of months before he's fully recovered."

"Really? Do you think he'll have to stay in hospital all that time?"

"Again, we're going to have to see what the doctors have to say. I suppose it depends on how quickly he heals and what damage he sustained to his head. I should think they'll be monitoring his progress daily with frequent CT scans."

"Poor Ben. He didn't deserve this. Those boys better pay for what they've done to him."

"It's going to be difficult to trace them if there were no witnesses to the crime. That's why we need to know what Ben can tell us or if there's any background information you can share with us. You've already told us that neither of you has encountered problems before, at school. Was that the truth, Josh?"

Again, his gaze landed on his brother before Josh answered. "Yes," he said, unconvincingly.

"I sense you're holding something back. It would be in everyone's interest if you told me the truth."

"I am. I'm not lying. Why would I do that?"

"Okay. We're going to leave now, give you some peace."

She closely evaluated his reaction then continued, "We have an appointment with Mrs Lowther at your school."

He stared at her, his eyes narrowing for a split second. "Okay. Will you visit Ben again soon?"

Footsteps sounded outside, and the curtain was drawn back to reveal Georgina. "Oh, hello. I was hoping I would bump into you, Inspector."

"You can call me Sam. How are you, Georgina?"

"Can I have a quick word with you, if you have the time?"

"We were getting ready to leave. We'll see you again, Josh. You've got my number, call me if you need me. Don't be afraid to ask for help."

"Thank you." His cheeks coloured, and his gaze flicked between Sam and Bob and finally landed on Georgina.

Sam shuffled closer to Ben and touched his arm. "Now you be a good boy and listen to the nursing staff, you hear me? I'll be back to visit you soon."

Ben's eyes fluttered shut and sprang open again, obviously fighting to stay awake.

"Get some rest," she ordered. "And, Josh, you should nip to the canteen, get something to eat and drink while Ben is having a snooze."

Bob slipped his hand into his pocket, removed his wallet and plucked a tenner from it. "This one is on me."

Josh's eyes widened. "Thanks, this is amazing."

They left the cubicle and walked towards the exit.

"Thanks for letting us see him," Sam said to the nurse. "I think Ben is going to have forty winks now and I believe we've persuaded Josh to go to the canteen."

"Ah, thanks for telling me."

In the corridor, the three of them found an area away from the ward, preventing Josh from overhearing their conversation if he appeared.

"Is everything all right?" Sam asked Georgina who flopped into the chair beside her.

"Do you want an honest answer or one I usually dish out when someone asks me that question whilst I'm on duty?"

"I only deal with honest answers, where possible. What's wrong?"

Georgina dropped her handbag on the floor behind her and swept her long brown hair into a ponytail. "Forgive me if I sound frustrated, it's because I am."

"About what?"

"After I rang you, I left the office and drove out to see Dora, the boys' aunt."

Sam inclined her head, not liking where the conversation was leading. "And?"

"And, you're never going to believe this. She was still tucked up in bed at ten-thirty in the morning, when her nephew's life might well be hanging in the balance."

"Before I let my mind run away with me, I need to ask if she is ill."

"No, she's as fit as a fiddle as far as I could tell. I asked her why she wasn't here, sitting with Ben. She told me it would be pointless as they had nothing in common."

"Nothing in common?" Sam repeated, aghast. "She's his damn aunt. How did you leave it with her?"

"I had to come down heavily on her, pointed out that she had a legal responsibility to care about him and that she should be here, while he's in hospital, at least until he's out of danger."

"Did that jolt her, make her reconsider her selfish behaviour?"

"I think it did, sort of. She then came up with a feeble excuse of having a migraine and told me she had a lunchtime appointment with her GP."

"Don't tell me you believed her?"

"I didn't feel like I had an option. I'm not in the habit of getting people's backs up, accusing them of blatantly lying to me. We have to tread a very fine line in that respect. As I'm sure you must do."

"You're right. I'm probably being unreasonable, but not as unreasonable as a guardian who is refusing to visit her nephew, suffering from a serious head injury."

"I'm with you, one hundred percent, hence my frustration."

"Do you want us to go round there? Do you think it will help?"

"I don't think so. I know thrusting two teenage boys on her at short notice needs to be taken into consideration. Maybe we should give her some slack. Time to reassess and do the right thing for the boys. I keep trying to put myself in her shoes but I'm finding it difficult. I'd have to be at death's door to swerve this place and to reject the boys' cry for help, especially as we keep saying, with them having to deal with the tragic loss of their father."

"Maybe we should give her twenty-four hours to reflect."

"I told her I would check in with her later, after she's visited the GP. I did tell her I was on my way here, giving her the option to ask for a lift rather than rely on public transport. It went straight over her head."

"Perhaps if she has got a migraine, maybe that's the reason behind her dodgy decision-making, and like you say, we should give her some leeway, for now."

Bob remained quiet during the conversation.

Sam nudged her knee against his. "Have you got an opinion on this matter, partner?"

"Who, me?" he asked, shocked that she should think to include him.

"Yes, you. That is, unless I've gained another partner in the last five minutes."

"Er... umm... no, not really. I think you and Georgina have pretty much covered all the options available."

Sam shook her head but then realised he had probably been lost in thought, trying to sort out his own problems. "Hmm... okay, I'm going to make the call. Bob and I will go over there now. Maybe the police showing up at her door will force her to rethink her position and start putting the boys first or at least consider their needs more."

"It can't do any harm. Thanks, Sam. Sorry to park this on your doorstep when you have enough on your plate already. I take it you will be looking into the assault on Ben?"

"Absolutely. Hey, going over there and interviewing the aunt is all part of the investigation, whether she appreciates us showing up at her door or not. If we go now, we should catch her in before she has to leave for her lunchtime appointment."

"Thanks. I'll just check on the boys briefly and get on my way again. I've got it in my mind that I should get a placement sorted out for the boys, just in case things turn sour with their aunt."

"I think I'd be inclined to do the same."

Georgina picked up her bag and stood. "Thanks for doing all you are for them. I'll be in touch soon."

"I'll give you a call later, let you know how we got on with the aunt."

"That'd be great. Good luck."

Sam blew out a breath. "Come on then, partner, we'd better get on the road. Are you all right?"

"Why shouldn't I be?" He marched up the corridor in front of her.

Sam jogged to keep up with his long strides. "Hey, talk to me. I only asked because you seemed to be in a world of your own back there."

"I have my own problems that I'm eager to sort out."

She clutched his arm, forced him to stop and face her. "If you want time off to speak with the head, you only have to ask. I can drop you off at the school en route and go to visit the aunt myself. How does that sound?"

He contemplated her suggestion for a moment or two and shrugged. "I don't mind, if you think you can handle the aunt by yourself. It might be better if we tackle her together."

"No, I'm getting the impression she needs to be treated with kid gloves. I also think if Milly's predicament is weighing heavily on your mind, there's only one thing left for you to do, deal with the situation head-on. The worst thing you can do is let things fester and work yourself into a tizzy."

"A tizzy? How would you react if you thought your daughter was being bullied?"

She raised her hands. "Hey, I'm not the enemy here." She continued to walk, left him mulling over the way he'd jumped down her throat. "Are you coming?" she called once she'd reached the lift.

He nodded and joined her. "Sorry."

The lift doors opened. They entered, and Sam pressed the GF button. Once the doors closed, she faced him and asked, "What are you sorry about?"

"For being an arse."

"I wouldn't necessarily call you that… er, there are times when I often think it, but not this time. I happen to think you're being a thoughtful and concerned father. Furthermore, I'm proud of you. There, I've admitted it out in the open for once."

"With no one else around," he mumbled.

She jabbed him in the arm with her clenched fist. "You're a card at times. I mean it, Milly should be extremely proud and grateful to have a father like you."

His head lowered, and he muttered, "Thanks."

The lift doors opened, saving him from any further embarrassment.

AFTER DROPPING Bob off at the school gates, Sam drove to the aunt's address on the other side of town. Sam had to admit, she didn't venture over this side often, through choice, only because she had no friends or family living out this way.

She knocked on the door of the small terraced house. It took a while for Dora Barstow to open it, and when she did, her blonde hair was messed up and she was still in her pyjamas and dressing gown.

Sam showed her warrant card. "Hi, I'm DI Sam Cobbs. Would it be all right if I came in to have a chat with you, Mrs Barstow?"

"What about?"

"The incident that put your nephew in the hospital."

She threw the door back. It smacked against the wall and almost bounced closed on Sam. "Come in, if you have to."

Sam eased the door open and entered the house.

Dora leaned against the doorframe to one of the rooms and folded her arms. "We can talk here. I haven't tidied up yet. I've been ill."

"Sorry to hear that. Nothing serious, I hope?" Sam added a smile, hoping to break through the icy atmosphere.

Dora unfolded her arms and rubbed her temples with her fingers. "Migraine. I haven't had one for years, then boom, this one struck out of nowhere. I shouldn't be surprised, not really, not after the upheaval I've been put through over the last couple of days."

"It must have come as a shock to you, to have Social Services knock on your door, asking you to take on the boys. You're to be admired."

"Ha, I'm only doing my duty, like any other decent human being would in the circumstances. I might not have seen eye to eye with my brother over the years, but there was no way I would have put his kids out on the street with nowhere to go."

"I'm sure I would feel the same if the issue ever arose in my family. Can I ask why you haven't visited Ben in the hospital yet?"

Dora rubbed at her temples again and closed her eyes. "Have you ever suffered from a migraine? The flashing lights, the nausea. Not being able to bear loud noises. It takes its toll on my body, I can tell you. I feel guilty for not visiting him, and I promise I will once I get rid of this damn headache, but I know I wouldn't be able to face going there when I'm feeling this bad."

"You have a doctor's appointment today, I believe."

"Has Georgina been in touch with you? Telling tales on me, has she?"

"Not at all. If anything, she was very concerned about you."

"Oh, sorry to have doubted her. Look, I know Josh is with his brother. He's only there for the day, before you start slating me for keeping him off school. I tried to make him see sense, send him off to school this morning, but he was having none of it, told me that he'd rather visit Ben instead. He's very close to his brother and extremely worried about him. I know I shouldn't have given in to his demands, but I felt if I didn't it would put a huge strain on our relationship before the boys and I have been given the chance to get to know each other."

Sam smiled. "Anything for a quiet life, eh?"

"That's what I was thinking. I swear, if I didn't have to deal with this blasted migraine, I would be at the hospital, by Ben's side, giving him the support he desperately needs. I believe I'm in a no-win situation, my health dictating what I can and can't do for my family right now."

"It's okay. I've told Georgina I will nip back to see Ben when I can. In the meantime, my team and I are going to be doing all we can to find the culprits who did this to your nephew. Has Josh opened up to you at all?"

She frowned and narrowed her eyes. "About what?"

"About if he saw the perpetrators or not? I know he was the first on the scene after the attack."

"No. He told me he found Ben and called for an ambulance right away because his brother was bleeding profusely. It must have been horrendous for him finding Ben like that. He was in a dreadful state when he came home."

"Did you go to the hospital last night?"

"Oh, no. I couldn't, my migraine was in full flow then. It has been raging since mid-afternoon yesterday, about three. I took myself off to bed then. Josh came home last night at around ten and went straight to bed. I called out to him, but he didn't respond. I thought it would be best to leave him; we're still trying to get to know each other. Taking tiny steps in our relationship. What's happened to Ben has been a huge shock to both of us. I feel so frustrated that I'm not well enough to visit him but, I know, from past experience, that I will only make the migraine worse by moving around and leaving the house. I'm better off in bed, trying to get rid of it. When I visit the doctor, he's likely to give me an injection to ease the symptoms. If it works, there will be nothing stopping me from going to the hospital later."

"I'm glad to hear it. Can you tell me, in the short time you've been reacquainted with the boys, if they've hinted at any possible problems at school?"

"Problems? With their schoolwork? You're not insinuating that they're illiterate, are you?"

"No, I wasn't referring to that side of things. I was asking if they'd mentioned if either of them had been subjected to any form of bullying."

Dora shook her head, winced and clutched her forehead in her hands. "Shit, I shouldn't have done that."

"My fault. I shouldn't be here, interviewing you when you're obviously not well. I apologise. It's just that the more information we can gather directly after an incident of this nature has taken place, the easier it will be for us to bring the investigation to a satisfactory conclusion."

"Do you know who the attackers were?"

"No. I've left my team trawling through the CCTV footage from all the cameras available in the area. I won't know what the results are until I return to the station."

"I see. Well, hopefully someone will come forward from one of the houses in that area. I can't believe no one witnessed the attack, not at that time of day."

"I'm inclined to agree with you. Listen, I'll leave you to get some rest and catch up with you another time. Sorry to have disturbed you. I hope the doctor can sort your migraine out for you today."

Dora smiled. "Thanks. It was good to meet you. The boys both spoke fondly about you the day Georgina dropped them off. Josh told me that you had treated them kindly after the death of their father. That was horrendous; any results from the post-mortem yet?"

"Not yet. But when my partner and I returned to the house, we found a suicide note hidden under a cushion on the sofa."

Dora gasped. "Really, can I see it?"

"It's been taken into evidence. I'll see if I can get you a copy in the next day or two. Saying that, I would rather keep it from the boys at this time. They're still processing their father's death and probably their mother's as well. I fear if they read the note or even had knowledge of its existence, it might do more harm than good. Plus, they have Ben's injuries and his recovery to deal with. I believe they've got too much on their plate already."

"What was in the note? Can you tell me that?"

"It was a heartfelt message from their father, pleading for their forgiveness for taking his life. He also wrote how much he missed the boys' mother. I think if they read it now, it's likely to set them back weeks, possibly months. Had they been a bit older, I wouldn't have any hesitation in showing it to them, certain they would be able to make the right call about its contents."

"I get that. I'm willing to take your advice on this issue. It's difficult for me to know what to do for the best in this situation, having drifted apart from the family over the years."

"I'm sure you're doing your best in the circumstances. Get well soon, thanks for chatting with me."

Dora smiled and showed Sam to the door.

CHAPTER 4

Sam drove back to the school but chose to remain in the car. She rang the station. "Hi, Claire, it's me. Has Nick passed you the extra information we need for the other two incidents that have happened in the area?"

"He has. We're going over everything now. Liam thinks he may have spotted the gang on one of the cameras. It was only a brief glimpse of a couple of youths on bikes, though. Nothing that we can call substantial evidence."

"That's a shame. Okay, have you got the details of the victims there? We'll call in and visit the parents, see if they can add anything else. Such as whether the boys have been bullied at school either before or after they were attacked."

"Do you want me to give you the information over the phone or shall I send you a text?"

"The latter, if you would. Thanks, Claire." She ended the call and texted Rhys to see if he was free for a chat.

He rang her a few seconds later. "I was just thinking about you. How's your day been so far?"

"Not ideal. How about yours?"

"Two no-shows and a woman who spent more time

crying and blowing her nose rather than actually speaking to me."

"Oh dear. Sounds like she was in a desperate state."

"She might have been. Unfortunately, I never got to find out."

"Are you telling me she didn't calm down and confide in you?"

"Far from it. It was her first time in a psychiatrist's office, and I think the pressure got to her. Ten minutes after her appointment started, she ran out of here saying, 'I can't do this. I don't know why I'm here. This isn't doing me any good, quite the opposite.' There's little I could have said or done to have changed her mind."

"Oh no, that wasn't much fun for you. Maybe she'll come back once she's had a chance to get her emotions in check."

"Perhaps. What's been going on with you, or shouldn't I ask? I have another appointment in ten minutes, so we're free to chat for a little while."

"Where do I begin…? No, I won't bore you with the details. I'll give you the bullet points instead."

He laughed. "I'm listening."

"You know the two boys I've had on my radar all week, after they lost their father?"

"I remember. Is everything all right with them? Didn't they go to their aunt's to live with her?"

"Full marks for having A1 recall. Seriously, the younger of the two brothers was admitted to hospital last night after being assaulted by a gang."

"Shit. How bad is he?"

"Bad enough. A few broken bones and a concussion to contend with."

"Ouch, poor lad. He had to endure one of the worst days of his life at the start of the week and now he has this hanging over him. What's the prognosis?"

"They think he'll be all right. They're sending him for regular CT scans to monitor the concussion. I can't help feeling that I've let him and his brother down."

"That's absurd. Don't you dare think that. You've bent over backwards for those boys in the short time you've known them."

"Hark at you. I haven't done that much for them, not really."

"You're being modest as usual. I wish I could help. Actually, I can. I should have chased it up yesterday. I sent my friend, Belinda, a message to ask if she could offer any advice for the boys and I've just realised she hasn't got back to me yet. I'll give her a call after I've seen my next patient."

"Thanks, any help will be gratefully received. I've got a few people to see this afternoon. Maybe we can discuss it further when we get home tonight. Here's Bob now. Remind me to tell you what's going on with him as well."

"Will do. Sounds like you've got your hands full today."

"You could say that. See you later, I should be home at the normal time. Love you."

"I'll pick up something special for dinner at lunchtime. Love you, too. I hope your day brightens up for you."

"Likewise." She blew him a kiss as the passenger door opened. She'd been trying to assess Bob's mood before he reached the car but found his expression unreadable. "Everything all right?" she asked once he'd slipped into his seat.

"You tell me because I'm none the bloody wiser."

"What's that supposed to mean?"

"I need a drink. I don't usually ask, but would you mind if we stopped off somewhere to have a decent coffee? I'll pay. I'd rather have a pint, but I take it that would be out of the question."

"Yep, not advisable while we're on duty. So caffeine it is. Where do you fancy going?"

"I don't care, I just need to get away from this effing place." His breathing was laboured, as if he'd just finished a half-marathon.

She switched on the engine. A café with several decent types of coffee beans on offer suddenly came to her mind. She completed a three-point turn and headed back into the centre. She found a parking space opposite the premises she had chosen.

"Have you been here before?" he asked, his eyes narrowing.

"Yes, my sister and I come here quite a lot, well, we used to, when we met up for our regular shopping expeditions. The coffee is amazing, it's going to blow your mind."

"Sounds perfect. I'm buying."

"We'll see. Chin up, matey."

"I'm fine. Angry, not depressed. I'll tell you more once I have a coffee in hand. I'm hoping it'll help me get rid of the bitter taste in my mouth."

"That bad, eh?"

They crossed the busy road, dodging the speeding traffic to get to the other side. He jumped back when a motorbike almost clipped his toes.

"Why isn't there a copper around when you need one?" Bob complained.

"We're definitely taking a risk. Maybe we should have used the pelican crossing fifty feet away from us like normal people tend to do."

"I couldn't be arsed," he said and grinned.

Sam ordered two speciality coffees off the board, accompanied by a piece of carrot cake for each of them. Despite Bob telling her this was on him, she pushed him away and handed over her bank card to the cashier.

"Thanks, you're as busy as ever, Paula."

"We haven't seen you for a while, Sam. How's Crystal

been? I dropped into her shop a couple of months ago. She was kind enough to give my cousin a discount on a beautiful wedding gown."

"She always looks after her friends well. When's the wedding?"

"Next month. Crystal is making some slight adjustments to the gown."

"Your cousin is in safe hands. And to answer your question, I haven't seen her for a few weeks. I need to rectify that. Time flies, and sometimes we need to jump off the merry-go-round and take time out."

"Sorry to hear about your mum. From what I can remember, she was a lovely lady. Crystal brought her in here a few times."

"Thanks. Life goes on. My parents had a good life together. I think Dad feels a little lost without her."

"He's bound to. I won't hold you up any longer, I'll bring them over."

"Thanks, Paula. Nice seeing you again, sorry it's been so long."

Sam picked up the necessary cutlery and serviettes from the serving unit at the end of the counter and joined Bob at the table he'd chosen by the window on the far side of the café. "Right, are you going to tell me what happened?"

He heaved out a breath and selected four sachets of sugar from the container in the middle of the table, then he proceeded to fiddle with one of the packets while he spoke. "She was like a different woman to the one we visited the other day."

Sam frowned. "Maybe she wasn't best pleased, you showing up out of the blue, without making an appointment first."

"Yeah, she made that perfectly clear. She started off okay, invited me to sit down. Maybe she thought I was there to give her an update on how Ben was doing in the hospital, that's the impression I got. But as soon as I revealed the true reason behind my visit, I swear her hackles surfaced right before my eyes."

"How strange. So, you told her what you suspected, that Milly was being bullied? What did she say in response to that suggestion?"

"She was adamant they didn't have a single bully at the school. That she ran a tight ship and never let tiffs between the pupils escalate into more than just that."

"Tiffs between the pupils? How can she be sure the school hasn't got a bullying problem? Hang on, before we tie ourselves into knots and accuse her of walking around with her eyes closed, to be fair, all the incidents that have been brought to our attention, including the attack on Ben, all happened off the school premises."

Paula delivered the drinks and pieces of cake and placed them on the table. "Can I get you anything else?"

"No, we're fine. Thanks, Paula."

"Enjoy."

Sam put two sachets of sugar in her coffee, and Bob poured four into his.

He stirred his coffee. "I know that, but it should be obvious because of the proximity of the attacks that they're related to the school."

"It comes back to something we work with every day in our job, evidence, or in this case, lack of it. I suppose you have to see this from her point of view, don't you?"

He put a forkful of cake in his mouth and chewed on it while he contemplated her question. "That's hard to do when it's your child at risk. Easier for an outsider to do, who doesn't have to deal with the consequences."

His words came at her with the full force of a dagger to her heart. "Sorry, I know I don't have kids, and while I appreciate what you guys are going through at this time, it would be irresponsible of me not to take into consideration the facts as we know them. Anyway, maybe this would be an ideal time to point out that you're only surmising that Milly is being bullied because she refuses to discuss the issue with you."

He stared at her. "What are you saying? That I've jumped in feetfirst before I knew what the real issue is?"

She shrugged and slipped another piece of cake into her mouth. After she'd swallowed it, she replied, "Maybe you're guilty of being overly officious on this issue."

"Thanks. I don't think I've ever been called that before. What makes you think my daughter's well-being is a trivial matter? Just asking."

Sam sat back and swirled her coffee in her cup. "All right, perhaps that wasn't quite the right word for me to use. What I'm trying to advise, clearly not well enough, is to take a step back. Try and sit down with Milly, preferably with Abigail there as well, and ask her outright if she's being bullied."

"If only it were that simple. Any parent will tell you that dealing with teenagers takes skill and diplomacy most of the time."

"I'm not saying it's going to be easy for you, but on the flip side of that, working yourself up into a state like this isn't going to help matters either, is it?"

"I thought it would make me feel better, you know, me doing something proactive about keeping my daughter safe. What I hadn't anticipated was coming up against a stubborn headmistress who is adamant her school hasn't got a problem with bullying."

"In this day and age, I do find that incredibly hard to believe, given the bullying statistics that are circulating the country at present. Maybe it's a case of her trying her best to push it under the carpet rather than deal with it head on.

Perhaps there's more going on with Lowther than meets the eye."

He frowned. "I don't get where this is leading."

"She's got a board of governors she has to keep happy, hasn't she?"

"Ah, yes. You're probably right. But how does that address the issue we've got?"

"It doesn't. I know this isn't what you're hoping to hear, but maybe you should do as I suggested, try and get the truth out of Milly about why her attitude has altered lately and go from there. Are you sure she hasn't got a boyfriend?"

"Christ, I hope not. That's yet another bridge we've got to cross one day. Right now, would be far too soon in my eyes."

"There's one option I think you should consider. Putting your detective skills to good use. That's the route I would take."

"In what way?"

"Search her room, see if you can find any clues."

"Christ, you really don't have a clue about teenagers, do you? Either that or you're guilty of living in the Dark Ages."

Sam pushed her empty plate away and wiped her mouth on a serviette. "Excuse me?"

"Kids, correction, teenagers, have rights these days. If we go hunting around her bedroom when she's not there and she finds out about it, I reckon she'd take the first steps to divorcing us."

Sam couldn't help laughing. "Is that you overexaggerating again?"

"Not at all. As I stated at the beginning of this conversation, you have no idea what it's like bringing up a teenager in today's world."

"Maybe that's true. If that's right, then I would suggest you avoid seeking my advice in the future, rather than us falling out with each other over this issue."

He cocked an eyebrow. "I won't, thanks for the advice. Are you ready to leave?"

"Not yet. I still have some coffee left. You've barely touched your cake."

"I've lost my appetite, not that I had much of one when we arrived."

"I'm sorry if this is a case of the truth hurting too much, Bob."

"No, you're right. It was foolish of me to come to you in the first place, to gather any nuggets of meaningful advice."

"Ouch, there's no need to say it like that."

He stood and tucked his chair under the table. "I'll meet you back at the car. I need to grab some fresh air all of a sudden."

"Bob, don't walk away from me," she pleaded, but he chose to ignore her.

He left the café and paused outside the front door to suck in lungfuls of fresh air then turned right.

Sam glanced over at the counter. Paula mouthed to ask if everything was all right. Sam nodded and mouthed, 'Men' and rolled her eyes.

Paula laughed. Sam stared at what was left of his cake and pondered whether to ask Paula for a doggy bag and take it with her, then decided he probably wouldn't want it anyway, not with the mood he was in.

She sat there an extra few minutes and then went in search of Bob. As she walked out of the café, she spotted him on the pavement on the other side of the road, going back to the car. He waved at her. The walk seemed to have done him some good as he appeared to be more relaxed than he was during their chat.

"Feeling better?" she asked when she was within a couple of feet of her car.

"I suppose so. I think the sooner I get my mind back on the job the better my mood is going to get."

"You said it. We'll visit the Grady family. Dean was the first boy to get attacked."

"The one who received minor injuries compared to the second boy?"

"That's right. Why don't you ring ahead? It'll be a waste of time for us showing up if the parents are out." She handed him her phone which she'd opened up on her text messages, in particular the one Claire had sent her.

Before he made the call, Bob input the Gradys' address into the satnav, and Sam pulled into the traffic when the next available gap came along.

"Hello, is that Mrs Grady? This is DS Bob Jones from the Cumbria Constabulary in Workington. I wondered if it would be convenient if my boss and I dropped round to see you… It would? That's great. We're about fifteen minutes away… Thank you, we'll see you shortly." He ended the call and exhaled a breath.

Sam patted his knee. "There, that wasn't so bad, was it?"

"I still reckon any calls should be made via the boss."

She laughed. "Another cop-out. Do you want to ring the Powells while you're on a roll?"

"Why not?" He prepared himself by sucking in a couple of breaths and letting them seep out slowly between his lips.

"It's a phone call, I'm not asking you to give up part of your pension pot."

"There's no need to bring that to the table."

"Sorry, I couldn't resist." She grinned. "Get on with it, we've got five minutes until we get to the Grady house."

"God, you can be super pushy at times." He punched in the number and sighed. "No answer."

"Okay, we'll try again after we've visited the Gradys."

. . .

MRS GRADY INVITED them into the kitchen of her detached house on a relatively new estate situated on the outskirts of Workington.

"I must say I was very surprised to receive your call. Can I get you a drink? I'm Felicity by the way. Mrs Grady seems far too formal for me to consider at this time of the day."

"We'll decline, if you don't mind, as we've not long had a coffee, but thank you. You said you were surprised when my partner called you earlier. May I ask why?"

They all sat at the round kitchen table.

"Because apart from your initial interest in my son's case, no one from the station has bothered to contact us, until today. Am I right in thinking your visit is to do with the investigation?"

"We believe so. Last night another boy was attacked by a gang of youths in the same area where Dean was attacked."

"Really? Do you know who these people are? Have they been caught?"

"Sadly, there were no witnesses. The victim is in hospital with very bad injuries. We've visited him, but he's got concussion, and the last thing we want to do is put him under pressure."

"I see. So, may I ask why you're here?"

"Once we put the details of the third attack into the system, it highlighted the other incidents that had occurred over the last six months, Dean's case and one other. According to our records, Dean told the investigating officer that he couldn't identify the people who attacked him. Has that changed in the last few months?"

Felicity shook her head. "No, if he had suddenly remembered anything I would have contacted the station and updated his statement." She placed her right hand on her cheek, and a sadness crept over her.

"Are you all right? I understand how upsetting all this must still be for you."

"I'm okay, but my son has changed beyond all recognition since the dreadful attack. He's twelve and appears to be living in fear every minute of the day. That's why you've caught me at home today, I've had to give up my job. I take him to school in the morning. He gets uptight if I'm not waiting around for him at the gates during break times, including lunchtime. It tears me apart to see him become a shadow of his former self, all because of what a group of thugs did to him." She swiped at the tears which dripped onto her cheek. "I'm sorry. I thought I was stronger these days but I'm obviously not. He's the baby of our family. The night he got attacked changed us all. My husband is angrier than I've ever seen him in twenty years of marriage. He lies beside me having nightmare after nightmare every night."

Sam reached for her hand. "I'm so sorry it has caused so much devastation within your family."

"It's something we all need to learn to cope with, but I can't imagine that ever happening."

"Have you tried counselling?"

"I want to do it. Hubby and Dean aren't too keen on the idea, though. My husband keeps telling me it's our problem and no outsider is going to come in and solve it for us."

Sam inclined her head. "He wouldn't do anything silly, would he? Like consider taking the law into his own hands?"

"Oh, goodness, no, I didn't mean that at all. He simply believes that if we keep the problem between the three of us, we can work things out for ourselves, given time."

"And how's that theory working out for you so far?" Sam smiled throughout, to soften her words.

"Well, between you and me, it's not. However, once Greg gets an idea into that head of his, there's nothing I can do to shift it."

"Which is why someone from outside the family should be given a chance. Your son was attacked back in January. Stating the obvious here, but bear with me, that's five months ago and, between you, you haven't managed to work things out yet. Don't you want to get back to work?"

"Yes, of course I do. I feel my life is being wasted, me sitting around at home. I know it's my responsibility to want what's best for my child but sometimes I sit here and wonder if we're possibly doing him more harm than good."

"Have you thought about changing schools?"

She looked down at her hands. "I did suggest that. Greg, on the other hand, thought it was a dumb idea. He's adamant he wants Dean to stay where he is because he went there, and they have an excellent reputation. None of the other schools in the area match their standards. I can see his point, but he doesn't see the way Dean is constantly peering over his shoulder during break times. I've seen him take stick off the other kids when he leaves me and makes his way back to the classroom. I'm not insinuating it's harsh bullying, it's just the odd child calling out 'Mummy's Boy' or something along those lines. To hear that, it crucifies me, and there's not a damn thing I can do about it." Fresh tears emerged.

"Please, try not to get too upset. We're here to help, not add to your worries."

"I think it's the relief overwhelming me, the fact that you're sitting here with me when I thought the police had cast us aside."

"In my colleagues' defence, it's difficult. Without more to go on there's very little we can do. That's why we rely on witnesses coming forward or the victim themselves remembering something of importance that happened during the incident."

"Good luck with that one. I believe Dean has blocked it from his mind, what he was subjected to that day, and who can blame him? You should have seen his reaction when he found out the second boy had been attacked. I thought he was going to have a seizure. I had to rush him to the doctor's. Thankfully, someone saw him as soon as I arrived in the reception area. They calmed him down, told me what to do in the event of him having further panic attacks. He's twelve, for Christ's sake. He shouldn't be dealing with shit like this. What sort of life is that for a boy of his age?"

"You're right, he shouldn't. It's totally unnecessary and horrendous for all your family to have to deal with."

"What about this latest attack? What can you tell me about it?"

"Only that the thirteen-year-old lad left school at home time; he was supposed to have waited at the gates for his brother, but he got bored and wandered off. We believe, although the victim has yet to tell us what the true sequence of events was on the day, it's likely that he was pounced on from behind. He was beaten black and blue, ended up with concussion, a broken nose and arm. We haven't been able to get too much information out of him yet because of the head injury. His brother is with him at the hospital."

"It's too terrible to comprehend, isn't it? Why pick on a young lad like that? These people need to be strung up for the damage they've caused, not just physically but mentally as well."

"I agree."

"You said the boy's brother was with him. Where are the parents?"

Sam sighed. "Sadly, they're both dead. Their father lost his life on Monday."

Felicity frowned. "May I ask how he died? Do you think there's a connection to the assault on his son?"

"I don't think so. The boy's father decided to end his own

life. He just couldn't cope with the loss of his dear wife; she died of cancer six months ago."

"Oh my, that's simply awful. What a tragic situation for the boys to have to deal with and now one of them is lying in hospital. Life can be so cruel at times, can't it?"

"You're not wrong. I believe the older brother will be strong enough for both of them. I have every confidence that he'll get them through this."

"How old is he?"

"Fifteen."

"That's a lot of responsibility for a boy of that age to have sitting on his shoulders. Are they living with a relative now?"

"An aunt has stepped in and offered them a home."

"That must have been a relief for the boys. I'm sorry, you must think I'm the nosiest person alive."

"Not at all. I would be asking the same questions you are if I were in your position. My concern is that if we don't find the gang responsible for the attacks and put an end to their cruel behaviour, they're only going to get a lot worse, possibly end up with a child losing their life."

"I can't promise anything, but all I can do is let my husband and son know that you've been here today and see if sharing the news about this latest attack will make enough of a difference with Dean for him to start opening up to us."

"That's all we can ask of you. I'll leave you one of my cards, please get in touch if anything comes to mind that your son feels would be helpful to our investigation. We'll get out of your hair now."

Felicity showed them back to the front door. "I promise I'll do my best."

"Thank you. It was nice to meet you, and please, don't be too hard on yourself. You've sacrificed a lot for the sake of your family."

"I know, but it's not about me, it's about Dean and

making him feel safe in his environment. I hope you capture the gang and get them off the streets. Knowing that they can't hurt him any more might be instrumental in allowing him to lead a normal life again. And dare I say it, we might all be able to get back to being a proper family again."

"Wouldn't that be great? I'll keep in touch with any progress we make."

"Thank you, I'd appreciate it."

CHAPTER 5

The bike drove towards him at speed. Josh leapt to the side, anger searing through his veins. Another bike hurtled towards him; he was ready this time. He stuck out an arm and knocked the rider off. He landed with a thump on his back and writhed around in pain. Josh thought about pouncing on the bugger and knocking seven bells out of him, but the other bikes kept coming at him, one after the other, each of the riders shouting in his face and kicking out as they passed.

"Did Daddy kill himself? Why? Because he was fed up with you and cry baby Ben?" One of the youths shouted.

Josh glared at him. Clenched his fist and waited for the opportunity for him to take the lad out. He didn't know the boys, but he had an inkling they were the ones from school who had made his life hell the previous year. But tonight, they were well disguised, dressed all in black and wearing clown masks.

He darted towards the boy still lying on the ground, desperate to get a look at the shithead, but another member of the gang realised what he was up to and drove at him, veering off to the right at the last minute. Josh's heart felt like it was on the verge of erupting from his chest. His breathing had become erratic as the anger built within him. He didn't care if he got hurt, all he wanted to do was get revenge for what these bastards had done to his younger brother.

"Daddy come to visit you, has he? From the afterlife, to check how your pathetic brother is doing?"

"I'll get you for hurting him. You're a bunch of cowards. Why didn't you come after me? Too scared, were you?"

"Do we seem scared to you, shit for brains?" One of the bikes came up behind him, and the thug kicked him in the back.

Josh fell face-first into a puddle beside the grassy patch nearby. Fearing what the thugs would do once he was lying defenceless on the ground, he bounced to his feet. His fists raised. "Think you can scare me, think again, arseholes."

There were five bikes in total. The riders all laughed and pedalled off. Josh took off, ran back to his aunt's house, constantly peering over his shoulder.

The second he entered the house, she was ready for him. He got whacked on the arm, hadn't seen the large saucepan coming at him until the last moment. It was aimed at his head, but his raised arm took the brunt of the force.

"Where the fuck have you been?" the evil bitch, as he preferred to call her, screamed at him.

"You know where I've been, at the hospital with my brother."

"I expected you home hours ago. Look at the state of you."

"I got set upon by a group of kids, the same ones who put Ben in hospital."

"How do you know that?" his aunt bellowed, getting right in his face.

His hands clenched and unclenched beside him. *Come any*

closer and I'll... He backed up and found himself pinned against the front door.

"I just do. There were five of them."

"Did they tell you they did it?"

"Not in so many words. They ribbed me about Dad's death as well."

"Haven't we all?" His aunt cackled like the witch she was.

Which made his blood boil even more. *You're pure evil. You're to blame for this. I wouldn't put it past you to have paid the gang to have Ben beaten up.*

She took a step towards him and poked his temple. "What's that little brain working on now, eh?"

"It's not. Leave me alone. I just want to get to my bed."

"It ain't going to happen. There are dishes to wash in the kitchen. Your tea is in the oven, if you want it. I want that kitchen sparkling before you go up to your room, you hear me?"

He nodded. Knew how pointless it would be to argue with her. The day they had arrived she had sat them down, made sure they knew the house rules. Told them they'd get a thrashing with the whip she had in her bedroom if they didn't comply.

For a peaceful life, he nodded and waited for her to stop glaring, grinding her teeth at him and take a step back. Then he walked into the kitchen. It was as if she had used every pot and pan in the cupboards. They were piled high on all the surfaces.

"What's all this?"

"It all needs cleaning. Do that first before you have your tea, it'll give you the incentive you need to complete the task quickly. I'll check in on you in ten minutes. Crack on, jump to it."

He shook his head.

"Are you refusing to do your chores? After the warnings I dished out the day you moved in?"

"Yes. You can't make me do it."

She caught him off-guard for the second time in five minutes. She grabbed hold of his right ear and twisted it. He'd never felt so much pain before and collapsed to his knees.

"What did you say?"

"Let go of me. Okay, I'll do it."

She cackled again. "I thought you might change your mind. Fucking teenagers, you think you know everything, don't ya? Well, I'm telling you that you know bugger all, my lad. You'll do what I say, when I say, got that?" She twisted his ear even more.

"Yes, I've got it. I'm sorry, I didn't mean to argue. Please forgive me?"

She pushed him away from her with such force, he cracked the side of his head on the edge of one of the base cupboards. He lay on the floor, dazed for several moments. She banged on at him, shouting in his face, telling him to stop pretending he was hurt, yelling at him to get up. Eventually, he got to his feet but had to pull himself upright using a nearby chair.

She didn't apologise for going over the top. Instead, she pushed him towards the sink and ordered, "Make sure the water is hot before you start, it's the only way you'll cut through the grease. After you've finished, have your tea and then go to your room. That'll teach you for bringing the police to my door. I warned you about that, didn't I?"

"Wait, what, the police were here?"

She folded her arms. "That's right, in particular that bitch turned up, the one you're keen on."

"What did she want?"

"It was a private conversation between me and her. Get

on with your work. If she shows up here again, I'm warning you, your punishment will be worse next time, am I making myself clear?"

"How is any of this my fault? I didn't ask her to come and see you. She was bound to check how we're settling in and if Ben was all right. She came to the hospital earlier, wanted to know where you were."

Dora swiped him around the head. He tried to duck but failed to avoid the blow in time.

"Don't talk back to me, I've warned you about that as well. Get on with the dishes, my soaps are about to start."

Through narrowed eyes, he watched her leave the room. If he hated her the first day they had arrived it was nothing compared to what was running through him now. *You'll get yours, you bitch! One day!*

Half an hour later, Dora popped her head around the door to check on him. By then, he'd washed and dried all the pots and pans and was in the process of wiping down the worktop.

"Good job. Don't forget to clean the oven and hob, they need a good scrub."

He opened his mouth to object but thought better of it. "Okay. It shouldn't take me too long."

"All the scourers are under the sink. Use the older ones first, they're still good for a few of the racks. I don't have waste in this house." She stomped back into the hallway.

I don't have waste... he mimicked. He emptied the bowl of mucky water and renewed it with fresh, only the fresh water was icy cold. He tried to clean the hob, but the grease smeared across the surface. Hesitantly, he left the kitchen and went into the lounge.

"What do you want? Have you finished it already? Do I need to come and inspect your work?"

"No, the water ran cold and it's not shifting the grease.

Maybe I can leave it until tomorrow when there's more hot water in the tank."

She glared at him, making him feel uncomfortable, giving him the impression he didn't belong there. He didn't, he knew that now.

"Leave it, have your tea and get to bed. I've seen and heard enough from you today. I'm sick to death of the sight of your miserable face."

Her vile words dealt him yet another painful blow. He should have been used to it by now. She hadn't said a kind word to either of them since they'd been forced to live with her. He left the room without replying and returned to the kitchen. He removed his dinner from the oven, cold baked beans on a slice of mouldy bread, the same meal he and Ben had been forced to endure since the day they had arrived. She'd spouted some excuse about not having the funds for a full shop at the supermarket. Josh had snooped in the cupboards, checked for himself; there was plenty in there. Items his mum and dad would have described as staple foods: rice, pasta, tinned tomatoes. There was cheese, eggs and milk in the fridge. Enough of the basics for her to cobble a decent meal together, if she could be bothered.

He ate half his meal then struggled to get past the bile wedged in his throat. He threw the rest of his poor excuse for a dinner in the bin, then rinsed his plate and cutlery under the tap, dried them and put them away.

I'm desperate for a drink. Could I sneak a glass of milk up to my room or some lemonade perhaps? Or should I ask her permission first?

He decided against the latter and removed a glass from the cupboard.

His aunt entered the room a moment later and caught him in the act. "What do you think you're doing, you greedy shit? What have I told you about using that much milk? You drink that tonight and you go without your cereal in the morning."

"But I'm thirsty, Aunt Dora. Please may I have some?" He hated the sound of his own whining voice.

"No, put the glass in the fridge and get to your room."

Reluctantly, Josh opened the fridge door and put the glass on the shelf at head height. He closed the door to find his aunt running a hand along the worktops, checking they were clean and free from fingerprints, except her inspection had created a plethora of prints, much to his annoyance.

"Do it again. It's not up to my standards. You're a filthy little shit who needs to learn how to clean things properly. I'll knock you into shape, given time." She laughed and walked out of the room.

He removed the antibacterial spray and cloth from under the sink and applied the liquid to the surface once more, scrubbing at the stubborn prints on the edge. He stood back to admire his work, shoved the cloth and spray under the sink again and left the kitchen.

On his way up the stairs, she walked out of the lounge and into the kitchen to inspect his work again. He paused, expecting her to shout his name. When silence filled the kitchen, he breathed out a relieved sigh and continued on his journey. At the top of the stairs, he entered the bathroom and helped himself to a glass of water. He detested the clear liquid, always had done, but there was nothing else available for him to drink, so what choice did he have?

The bruise on the side of his head had developed quickly. He touched it. It stung, caused him to wince. What had his life come to? Forced to live with the cruellest of people. His brother in hospital; he had no idea how long he was going to be there. The gang causing problems for him not far from his home. He brushed his teeth, washed himself in cold water and went to bed. Josh was exhausted. He fell asleep quickly until his aunt came to bed and slammed the doors to the bathroom and her bedroom. She didn't check to see if he was all right, like his parents used to. He missed them so much.

He raised his head off the pillow. He couldn't hear his aunt moving around so presumed she was asleep. He switched on the bedside lamp and removed the notebook and pen from under his mattress. After reading through what he'd written the previous night, he spent the next hour adding to the notes. He jotted down a to-do list that would need to be fulfilled before his plan could be actioned. Josh was aware that he would need to bide his time, ensure all the pieces were firmly in place before any of it could come to fruition. However, his main priority still remained with Ben. His brother's recovery was paramount, and everything else could wait until he'd been given the results of the scans.

The gang of youths would be shaking in their boots by the time he'd finished with them, if they survived. *Sod it, I'm that wound up, I'm not going to get any sleep tonight. I might as well get out there now and make a start.*

He crept around his bedroom, collecting the darkest clothes he could find and slipped into them. He chose a hooded sweatshirt, knowing that he would be able to hide his identity from the boys. Keen to get out there, Josh opened the window and slid out onto the roof of the kitchen extension below. This side of the house was lacking in streetlights, therefore the chances of him being seen were virtually zero, an added bonus to his plan.

He slid down the slightly sloping roof and landed on the concrete path below. There, he paused in case keen ears had heard his movements.

Unlikely, stop being so jittery and get your arse into gear.

He was aware of where one of the boys lived, who had bullied him in the past, it was just around the corner. He'd only been in less than an hour, so if he could get to his house, see if there was any sign of a bike in the back garden, he'd be sorted. He would class that as the first piece of the puzzle in his audacious plan and be jubilant with the result. He tiptoed to the end of the alley, cursing when a dog barked in one of the neighbouring gardens. He upped his pace and before long he was seconds away from Leo Burke's house.

Josh decided to hide for a couple of minutes to assess the new area. What he hadn't anticipated was there being a pub on the corner and the activity which surrounded it at this time of night. He did his best to stay tucked behind the pub's large commercial skip. At one point he glanced up and realised that any movement he made from now on was going to possibly be caught on CCTV.

Shit, I didn't even think about that. What do I do now?

He didn't have time to re-evaluate because a bike rounded the corner. It was easily recognisable as one of those that had been used by the gang. There was a large shark sticker on the strut of the handlebars. Josh pulled his hood forward to cover his features. He darted across the street and surprised the boy as he opened his back gate.

"Fucking scum. You deserve this for what you did to my brother." He jabbed the knife he'd stolen from his aunt's house into the boy's stomach.

Burke clutched the blade sticking out of his gut. He lacked any vocal communication. No scream, no swearing, absolutely nothing except a grunt when Josh removed the knife and wiped the blade across the boy's face and then his sleeve. In slow motion, Burke sank to his knees. He reached out a hand to Josh, seeking help. Josh kept a close eye on his surroundings, willing the boy to die; his aim was to see the fucker take his last breath. Seconds later, his wish was granted.

Josh knew how to check someone's pulse. Euphoria rose and surged through his veins and guided his steps back to the house. The only problem facing him now was how he got back to his bedroom without alerting either his aunt or the close neighbours.

Fuck, I didn't think this through properly, did I?

He opened the gate to the back garden and tested the bins to see which was the lightest to move. Luckily, it was the sturdiest of the three. He tipped it back, wheeled it into the alley and closed the gate behind him. It would confuse the hell out of his aunt if she found it there in the morning, unless the opportunity came his way to return it before she noticed.

Yes, that's what I'll do. Now I need to get my arse into gear and back to my bedroom before someone comes along and spots me breaking into the house.

That consideration fuelled his movements until he could release the breath he'd been holding in, once he was safely back in his bedroom.

He only just made it before a man and his dog, a neighbour from one of the houses backing onto his aunt's, entered the alley at the top.

Josh darted across the bedroom he shared with his brother, avoiding the creaky floorboards in the centre of the room and quickly undressed. His door was still closed, so as far as he was concerned his aunt probably hadn't come looking for him, not that he thought that idea was ever on the table.

He left his clothes in a pile on the floor with the intention of dealing with them in the morning and hopped back into bed.

One down... another four to go. It was quite simple really. The key is to catch the victim unaware, just like they'd done to Ben. Revenge will be all the sweeter if I can kill the fuckers over the next couple of nights.

He was delighted that his mind was free from any kind of remorse. Only a sense of achievement lingered until he closed his eyes and drifted off to sleep.

CHAPTER 6

On the way into work the following day, Sam revisited the interview she'd had with Laura and David Powell, the parents of the second boy who had been attacked a few months earlier. They were still more than a little irate about the involvement of the police, or lack of it, especially Mr Powell who had marched towards her and poked her in the chest. The movement had caught both Sam and Bob off-guard. Despite the delay in reacting, Bob made up for it. He overpowered the man and twisted Powell's right hand up his back then slammed him against the wall in the hallway of their small Victorian house.

David Powell ended up breaking down, ashamed of his behaviour. Sam had taken pity on the man who was understandably living on the edge.

After that initial outburst, the couple had invited them into the lounge and, together, went over the details as they knew them about the assault on their son who was, to this day, still extremely traumatised and had been known to take the odd day off school due to anxiety.

Although it was gone five when Sam and Bob had showed

up at the residence and Mark Powell was home from school, the parents felt it was best if they left their son out of the conversation. Sam agreed, with the proviso that they would be able to interview Mark in the near future.

The parents then laid all the facts on the table for them. Mark had been fourteen at the time. He'd celebrated his fifteenth birthday the week before their visit—maybe *celebrated* was an exaggeration in this case. The evening of the assault, Mark had just said farewell to a group of his friends at the bus stop a few streets from their school. He had been distracted, listening to music through his AirPods. His father had shaken his head and expressed his frustration at his son's lack of awareness of his surroundings that night. Had Mark heard someone coming up behind him he would have been prepared, ready to have put up a fight, according to his father.

Instead, Mark had been knocked to the ground by the youths. The rest was just a blur as he'd been rendered unconscious by a blow to the head from a heavy object, possibly some kind of solid bar. A couple of schoolchildren discovered him a while later. They had all stayed behind for an extra rugby class after school. They were the ones who had called the emergency services to attend the scene. The ambulance arrived, along with the police. Mark had been whisked off to hospital where they'd discovered the true extent of his injuries. Concussion and three fractured ribs, and boot marks had been discovered on his clothes by his father. The thugs had also broken both of Mark's legs.

At this stage, Laura Powell had needed to be comforted by her husband, and both parents clung to each other for support.

David Powell revealed how damaging that night had been for their family. Their son had since become seriously withdrawn. He'd refused point-blank to open up to either his parents or the police. His father believed Mark was concerned about the repercussions he might encounter if he did reveal what had happened that night. Therefore, his parents sought counselling for their son. At first, he'd rejected the notion of seeing a specialist, insisting that over time he would be able to cope, but his parents feared nothing would be further from the truth. Most of all they were worried about their son's mental health. One day, a couple of weeks after their son had been discharged from hospital, Laura cleaned Mark's room. There, hidden inside his pillowcase, she had discovered four packets of paracetamol. Between them, the parents decided not to confront their son about the tablets. Instead, they chose to remove them from his room, but the incident had left them wary of their son's every move. They both found it soul-destroying that they no longer trusted their son. Hence all of them living on the edge since the assault had occurred.

Sam had asked if the parents would allow her to speak with Mark over the next day or two. Reluctantly, after some additional persuasion from Sam, they agreed and told her to come back at the beginning of next week, giving the parents time to work on their son in the meantime.

Sam drew into her space at the station. She locked her car and was on the way to the main entrance when Bob arrived and blasted his horn.

"Morning. How are things with you this morning?" he asked.

"I'm okay. Glad to see you here. I had my doubts whether you'd show up after yesterday's outburst." She smiled, sensing that he was in a far better mood than he'd been in the day before.

At the end of their shift, they'd returned to the station after interviewing the Powells, and he'd lashed out at the furniture in the incident room. It had taken Oliver and Liam grabbing both of his arms to calm him down. Sam had then taken him into her office and read him the riot act.

"How many more times am I going to have to go over this with you, Bob? You need to let it go. Not become too involved in this issue."

He'd remained quiet for the next ten minutes, after she'd lectured him, then he'd stormed out of the office, gathered his jacket off the back of his chair and bolted from the incident room. Sam had sent Liam after him, but Bob had already driven off.

However, now, as they walked through the main entrance of the station, a sensation of doom and gloom hit Sam with full force.

At first glance, she could tell Nick wasn't his usual cheery self. The reception area was empty, no members of the public raising complaints. However, six uniformed officers were bearing the brunt of the desk sergeant's anger, or that's how it seemed to Sam.

"I want this stamped out. Now. Go on, you know what to do. Don't let me down."

Sam and Bob took a step back to allow the six officers to pass them on the way out of the station.

"Sorry you had to witness that, ma'am. I'm a tad wound up this morning."

"I can see that. What's up, Nick? You never let work get on top of you."

"I know." His chest pumped in and out.

"You're going to cause yourself a heart attack if you don't calm down."

"I'm all right now. It's been full on since I got here at six. I toyed with the idea of calling you but thought better of it."

Sam frowned and cast a concerned glance towards Bob. Then she asked Nick, "You've got me intrigued now. What's going on?"

"We had reports about a stabbing last night. The boy was dead when the patrol turned up. His father found him in the alley at the rear of their property."

"A boy? How old?"

"Fifteen."

Sam rolled her head back and hissed. "Not again. And yes, you should have called me, Nick."

"Sorry, I realise that now. At the time I didn't think there would be anything you could do to help because it was a fatality. It wasn't until I really thought about the incident that I made the possible connection."

"Don't worry about it, what's done is done. The pathologist, was he called to the scene?"

"Yes, all that side of things was actioned last night. The scene is clear now. When I say clear, I mean the body has been transferred but SOCO are still in attendance."

"And the parents? I'm not going to ask how they are, that would be tactless. Have they given a statement?"

"No, they were too upset to give one last night."

"Understandable. How have you left it with them?"

"They asked us to delay the interview for a few days, until they've got their heads around their son's death."

"While I agree that's a good idea, it's not going to help us get the investigation underway, is it?"

"We're between the Devil and the deep blue sea. I'll give them a call after lunch, see how the land lies."

"Tread carefully would be the only piece of advice I can give you on that one, Nick."

"I will. In the meantime, I've dispatched my team to conduct the house-to-house enquiries in the area."

"I was going to ask if you've arranged that yet. Thanks. I'll give the pathologist a call, see what he can share with us at this stage." Sam smiled. "Why don't you get a cup of coffee down your neck and chill for ten minutes?"

"You read my mind."

Sam punched her security number into the keypad, and the door sprang open. During their journey up the stairs, she couldn't help but notice how quiet Bob was behind her. "Everything all right?" she called over her shoulder.

"I'm thinking."

"I thought I could smell something."

"Uncalled for. I'm conscious of the fact of watching what I say. The last thing I need right now is you jumping up and down on my neck for passing unwarranted judgements or making daft statements about that damn school."

She laughed. "You're learning. No, seriously, we're going to need to study the facts first before we make any kind of assumptions."

"Which is what I said."

Sam reached the top of the stairs and turned to face him. "All I ask is that you do your best to keep your anger at bay on this one."

"In other words, you're expecting me to be the utter professional, even though the school and the issue of bullying keeps getting highlighted."

She raised a finger and wagged it. "That's you jumping to conclusions again. We don't know that for sure, not yet."

"Let's hope the pathologist can fill in the gaps for us."

"You get the coffees organised and I'll call him before I tackle my daily emails and post."

"I think I've got the better end of that deal."

"You definitely have." Sam walked in and wished the other members of the team good morning and continued into her office. Ignoring the view that usually drew her eye first thing, she sat and rang Des' number. "Sorry to call you so early. Can you speak?"

"I wish I knew who I was speaking to. I know I possess

great skills, but I should inform you that my psychic powers are lacking somewhat."

"My mistake, Des. Although I think you're winding me up. It's Detective Inspector Sam Cobbs calling."

"Ah, the inspector calls. How the dickens are you?"

"Cut the crap, I'm not in the mood for it. What can you tell me about the body you were called out to last night?"

"It depends on what you want to know."

Sam covered the mouthpiece of her phone and growled, then removed her hand again and said, "I'm open to what you want to give me, the more the better, if we're supposed to get the investigation underway this morning."

"Ah, yes. Very well. I'm about to start the PM in half an hour or so. Why don't you join me? I haven't had the pleasure of your company down here for a while. I can run through things with you then."

"Okay, you've twisted my arm. I'll be there in thirty minutes."

"See you later."

Sam ended the call and booted up her computer. Bob entered the room and deposited her mug on the desk.

"No answer?" he asked.

"It was the briefest of calls which ended with him requesting our attendance at the mortuary."

"A great way to start our day. I feel a happy dance coming on… not."

Sam laughed. "I told him we'll venture over there in half an hour, just enough time for us to finish our drinks. See, I do consider your caffeine levels sometimes, despite what you believe to the contrary."

"Whatever."

She whizzed through her emails and the few brown envelopes sitting in her tray and sipped at her coffee at the same time. In the end she was pleased and surprised how quickly she completed the chore compared to other mornings.

I could get used to this. I'm usually stuck behind my desk for at least a couple of hours in the morning. Could things be looking up on that front, or is it a case of head office having an off day and me capitalising on it?

She smiled at the thought and finished off the remains of her coffee.

DES WAS ready and waiting for them in his theatre. Sam and Bob were suited and booted in their gowns and wellies. Bob chose to wear a mask.

Sam rolled her eyes. "Wuss."

"No, I'm being practical."

Des got to work as soon as they joined him and performed the Y-section on the corpse.

Sam averted her eyes until the procedure was completed.

Des made the assessment of the victim's body for the recording as he worked his way down the corpse. It wasn't until he reached the fatal wound in the boy's stomach that Sam really took notice of what he was saying.

"I can only see one wound; I would expect there to be more. We rarely see a solitary wound in attacks of this nature. That's not me tarring every perpetrator with the same brush, but if you're going to attack someone in the street, past experience tells me it's generally a frenzied attack."

"Maybe the killer's intention was only to injure the boy and not kill him," Sam suggested.

"Possibly. It's hard to judge how long the victim was lying there unconscious. The wound was larger than normal. Therefore, he probably bled out."

"Reading between the lines, like I have to with you sometimes, what you're saying is you think he could have been saved?"

"More than likely, if he'd been found sooner."

"And there are no other wounds on him? He wasn't knocked out? I'm not doubting what you're telling us, I just find it incredible to believe a wound to the stomach resulted in his death."

"No wounds to the head at all. My expert opinion is that the victim died from a solitary knife wound."

Sam shook her head in disbelief. She'd encountered several victims with similar wounds over the years who had spoken to her, sitting up in their hospital beds, after they'd survived such an assault. "I'm struggling to get my head around this. Was a vital organ struck?"

"Yes, his liver. I'm calling it: had this young man been discovered earlier, I believe his life would have definitely been saved."

Sam struggled to take it all in. As if it wasn't bad enough to conceive this boy's life had been taken cruelly by someone, the fact that if he'd been found earlier he might still be alive today threw her head in a spin. "Are we done here?" she asked, almost choking on the bile rising in her throat.

Bob placed a hand on her arm and asked, "Are you all right, Sam?"

"Not really is the honest answer. I need to get out of here. Sorry, Des, I know this isn't ideal."

"Go. I'm used to it."

She left the theatre with Bob right behind her.

"Hey, I'm usually the one who has to deal with the queasiness, not you. What's going on?"

Sam stripped off her gown and threw it in the bag in the corner. "This has nothing to do with me feeling sick at the sight of the body being cut open, it's more to do with the injustice of it all. Without wishing to repeat what Des and I both said in there, the fact that had the lad been discovered earlier..." Her voice trailed off, she was fed up with repeating the same statement over and over.

Bob removed his gown and nodded. "I hear you. The truth is, we don't know how long he was lying around injured before he took his last breath. The wound was pretty big, possibly made with a large kitchen knife. There are too many variables: the width of the blade, the ferociousness of the attack, how deeply the knife penetrated. For what it's worth, the boy might have lasted five minutes or a couple of hours. We're never going to really know the truth, are we? I doubt if Des could even supply us with an accurate timeframe."

She ran her hands through her hair. "I know. I'm probably being foolish. Ignore me, the sooner we get to speak to the parents the better."

"Well, we know that's not going to happen today. It might be worth you giving them a call to add a bit of pressure, just saying."

"I was wondering the same. Yes, I'll do it from the car. We can't go any further until we get all the facts, can we?"

By the time they had reached the car, Sam declared herself back to normal. With her emotions now under control, she announced, "I'm just going to go for it."

"Huh? What are you talking about?"

"I'm going to call in to see the parents. Make out we were in the area. I know I'm taking a risk, could end up with a complaint against me, but surely, any parent in their situation would be desperate to find their son's killer, wouldn't they?"

Bob attached his seatbelt. "Absolutely. Maybe they weren't thinking straight at the time. I agree, we should head over there now."

"Can you ring the station? Speak to Nick and get the address from him. I'll head back into town."

Bob rang the station and put the phone on speaker. Sam could tell Nick was a bit put out by the request and was reluctant about handing over the address.

After he ended the call, Bob said, "Well, that royally pissed him off."

"Shit happens. We're the ones on the frontline. If the brown stuff is going to hit the fan, we're the ones who are going to get covered in it."

"Jesus... why say that? It's going to be tough to get rid of that damn image from my head now."

Sam laughed. The Burkes' house was a ten-minute drive from their location. Before getting out of the car, she issued Bob with some ground rules. "Any hassle and we make our excuses and leave, okay?"

"Hey, you're the boss, what you say goes."

Sam grinned. "If only you remembered that some days."

"Bloody cheek. I'm fully aware of my place in this relationship."

They laughed and left the car.

"Game faces back on. Let's hope they're willing to see us."

Bob rang the bell. They both had their warrant cards out, ready to show as soon as someone appeared.

A man in his early forties with greying hair at the sides opened the door moments later. "Yes?"

"Sorry to trouble you, Mr Burke, I'm DI Sam Cobbs, and this is my partner, DS Bob Jones. Is it convenient for us to have a word with you and your wife, sir?"

"Not really, no. We're both very upset. I told your lot to leave it a few days before you came round here, hounding us for information. I sent that FLO woman away too. We're entitled to this time to mourn the loss of our son just like any other family, aren't we?"

"You are indeed. The thing is, any information you can supply us with at this time could be crucial to our investigation."

"How?" he snapped.

"The longer we leave it the more likely it is that your son's killer will go on to either possibly maim or kill someone else. Most families reach out to us not long after they've lost a child or loved one, in the hope they can prevent other families being put in the same situation."

"Who is it, Dan?" a female voice filtered down from upstairs.

"It's the police. I'm dealing with it."

"I'll come down," his wife shouted back.

"No, stay there. I told you, leave this up to me to deal with." He returned his attention to Sam. "Everyone is different. My wife and I want to be left alone at this time. It's up to you to get on with your job and to stop hounding us."

"I appreciate how upset you must be right now and I'm sorry if you think we're hounding you. I can assure you we're not here to do that, far from it. All we're trying to get to are the facts behind your son's death."

"Let them in, I want to talk to them." A woman appeared behind Burke. She was shielding the side of her face with her hand, which instantly raised Sam's suspicions along with the hairs on the back of her neck.

"Thank you, Mrs Burke." Sam put a foot over the doorstep.

Burke puffed out his chest. He leaned forward, getting in her face, and shouted, "I said no and I meant it."

His breath reeked of alcohol. Sam turned to Bob and raised an eyebrow. "Mrs Burke has invited us in, sir, can you step aside, please?"

"I won't. My house, my rules."

Mrs Burke's hand slipped from her face to reveal a black right eye.

"Step aside, sir," Bob said. "Either that or we take this down the station, the choice is yours."

"Let them in… now, Dan. There's no point putting this off. I want this over and done with."

Mr Burke growled, turned and barged past his wife.

Sam entered the house and placed a hand on Mrs Burke's forearm. "Are you okay? Did he do that to you?"

"Yes. I don't blame him, he was upset." Mrs Burke sniffled.

"Upset? So he lashed out at his wife? How often does this kind of thing happen? Is that why he refused to be interviewed?"

Mrs Burke nodded.

"Please, you mustn't think badly of him. He gets wound up and…"

"Thumps his wife? We can take him in for assault. You only have to say the word."

"No, I don't want that. It was an accident. We were both distraught about Leo, and neither of us could sleep."

"Ha, usually husbands comfort their wives in situations like this, not knock seven bells out of them."

"I'm fine, truly I am. I don't want to make an issue about it. Come through to the lounge. Can I make you both a drink?"

"Thank you. My partner can make the drinks, if you like?"

"No, I'd better do it. He can't stand strangers helping themselves in our kitchen."

"In that case, we'll leave it. Sounds to me like he has a problem with a lot of things. I'm sorry this happened to you at this sad time. You know he's in the wrong, don't you?"

"I do. I just want to move on with my life and put all this behind me. Will you allow me to do that?"

"Of course. If you're telling me this was a one-off. Was it?"

She lowered her head and grasped her hands in her lap.

Sam sat on the sofa next to her. "You don't have to put up with this. There are people out there who will help you. Places you can go to seek refuge."

Mrs Burke shook her head. "Why should I leave the home I love?"

Sam inclined her head. "What's the alternative? For you to end up at A and E, or worse still, end up in the mortuary, alongside your son?" She regretted the words as soon as she'd said them. It didn't matter how true they were in her mind, she should have held her tongue.

"How can you say that? It would never come to that."

"How do you know? Answer me one question, I need the truth."

Mrs Burke nodded.

"Did your husband kill your son? Did Leo come home, see you two fighting and try to defend you?"

Shocked, Mrs Burke jumped to her feet. "How dare you even think that? Our son was killed by a warped individual, and here you are, sitting in my house, accusing my husband."

Sam raised her hands and patted the seat beside her. "I'm sorry, please sit down. You have to understand how bad this all seems to a copper. All I'm trying to do is get to the bottom of what happened to your son last night. Are you willing to tell me?"

"Yes, I want everything out in the open. We have nothing to hide... except this, and you're aware of that now." She pointed to the colourful bruise.

Bob removed his notebook from his pocket and poised his pen ready.

"I went to bed quite early, at around nine. I wasn't feeling too well. I think I ate something that didn't agree with me at lunchtime."

"Sorry to hear that. Was Leo at home?"

"No, he liked to meet up with his friends at night. They go out on the bikes, all good fun. I never mind as it's an excellent form of exercise. It's better than him sitting in his bedroom, playing with that PlayStation of his like other kids of his age. As long as his homework is done, it shouldn't matter, should it?"

"I agree. Life's too short for kids not to be out in the fresh air enjoying themselves. Did you set a curfew for your son?"

"I've always told him to be home by ten at the latest. I usually wait up for him, but last night was the one night I let him down. I took a tablet to help me sleep through the night, and it did the trick. I was asleep five minutes after my head hit the pillow."

"And where was your husband? Sorry, I didn't catch your name?"

Her gaze drifted to the door. Sam sensed she was checking it was still closed and that their conversation couldn't be overheard by her husband.

"It's Grace. He was… at the pub until late."

"How late?"

"After twelve. He stayed behind chatting to a group of friends."

"Which pub?"

"The Lion and Lamb at the end of our road."

"Within staggering distance of home. Makes sense for him to go there. Didn't you tell the officers who were first on the scene that your husband was the one who found your son?"

"That's right."

"Can you give us an exact time?"

"A little after twelve. I can't give you a definite time, and there would be no point asking Dan because he was too drunk to notice."

"A rough time is fine. So, your husband found your son and then what?"

"He came running into the house, shouting that something was wrong with Leo and I needed to call for an ambulance. Because of the sleeping tablets I'd taken, it took me a few minutes to come around. I asked him what he was talking about. He ran out of the house. I put my dressing gown on and followed him into the back garden. I found him standing over Leo's still body. My baby... he was just lying there, blood pouring out of his stomach. One look at him and I knew it was too late for us to try to save him. But there was no way I would stand back and not try. I pushed past my husband, got down on my knees and checked for a pulse in Leo's neck. His eyes were wide open, just staring into space..."

"It's okay, take your time. You're doing really well, Grace."

The door opened, and Mr Burke entered the room. Bob placed his notebook on the floor beside him, anticipating trouble.

"What have you said to her?" Mr Burke shouted. "Leave our house immediately. You were told to give us space for a reason. Neither of us is coping very well with the loss of our son. You shouldn't be here, forcing us to talk about this. I'm going to make a complaint to your senior officer."

"No, we won't do that, Dan. These people are trying to help us. Don't make this all about you and your needs. What I want or *need* has to be taken into consideration, too. Sit down and be quiet."

He sat on the edge of the single leather chair and placed his forearms on his thighs. "I can't believe he's gone. We want our son back." His voice, full of emotion, caught in his throat.

His wife shuffled along the sofa to sit next to him. She

covered his hands with hers. "That's not going to happen. We need to speak to the police. If we don't, it could set the investigation back. This way, they'll get a clearer picture and hopefully a witness will come forward with vital information."

"Okay. I'll see how it goes, but it's still raw for me. Hard to take in. I was the one who found him. It was the last thing I expected to see at that time of night."

"Did you see anyone else around at the time?"

"No one at all. I walked home from the pub, and I didn't see or hear anyone. We don't know how long he'd been lying there. That's what we're struggling to get our heads around, aren't we, Grace?"

"All of it has had an impact on us. The way he died, the fact that someone chose to kill him. Why? What harm can a boy of his age do or say to anyone for them to want to stab him?"

"Are you aware there has been a spate of attacks on schoolchildren in the past few months?"

The couple stared at each other and shook their heads.

"No, this is the first we've heard about it," Grace replied.

"What are you saying? I can't quite figure out what you mean. Are you saying that someone is setting out with the intention of hurting these kids, or do you think there's more to it than that?"

"Possibly. We're investigating an attack which happened a few nights ago, a young lad beaten up by a gang of youths who ended up in hospital. He's still there now. We also believe there's a connection to a few older cases that came to our attention from a couple of months ago."

"I can't believe what I'm hearing," Dan said. "Why haven't you caught the buggers? Got them off the streets by now?"

"It's only been a few days. The older cases didn't go anywhere because neither of the boys was willing to give us any details about the people who'd attacked them. Without that significant information… we're screwed, sorry, it's harder for us to get anywhere."

"And now that our son is dead? Surely, you're going to be in the same boat, or am I missing something?" Dan asked.

"Again, we're going to be relying on witness statements, if your neighbours either heard or saw anything. Have any of them mentioned anything to you at all?"

He shook his head. "We're hated around here, so I doubt if they would speak up even if they knew anything."

"Sorry to hear that. We have officers out there now, going house-to-house."

"I think that's probably going to be a drain on your resources," Grace said. "What my husband said is true. I don't think we're alone, it's the lack of sense of community we have these days. My neighbour used to care for our dog during the day, you know, let it out when we were at work all day, but then Sonia moved away, and when the new ones moved in, they ignored us from day one. If I could leave the estate I would, but Dan doesn't want to."

Sam faced Mr Burke. "May I ask why?"

"Because my local is at the top of the road. I've got plenty of friends up there from the other end of the estate. I couldn't give a toss about the fuckers living down this end, none of them are worth it."

"I see. Can you tell us who your son hung around with?"

The couple fleetingly glanced at each other.

"No, sorry. Our son wasn't the talkative type," Grace said. "You know what teenagers are like. They're at that stage between being a child and an adult. Rebellious about everything, no matter how minor it is. I was okay with Leo going out every evening. Sometimes he completed his homework before going out and other times, he'd finish it when he got home. As long as it was done, I didn't care."

"And you can't give us a single name to follow up on?" Sam asked, her heart sinking.

"No, sorry. If you have kids, you know how secretive they can be, or maybe that's the wrong word. Reluctant to share the ins and outs of their days with you. He was fifteen going on twenty-five, preferred to keep himself to himself."

Out of the corner of her eye, Sam noticed Bob nodding. "I don't have any, but my partner has a teenage daughter. What school did Leo go to?"

"Pittman's High School," Grace said.

"Thanks, we'll drop by and see the head."

"What about the other boys who were attacked?"

"They attended the same school."

"How strange," Grace said.

"Do you think someone is targeting the children from that particular school?" Dan asked.

"I think we'd be foolish to dismiss the notion. We've already spoken to Mrs Lowther this week. She's denied the school has a bullying problem."

"Hmm… what if the person responsible doesn't go to Pittman's? What if they go to a different school in the area? I'm trying to think outside the box."

"I'm not willing to rule anything out at this stage. We'll do some extra digging. Is there anything else you can tell us?"

The couple shook their heads.

"I think we've told you everything," Grace said.

"Can I say something?" Dan asked, his voice shaking.

"Of course," Sam replied. She studied the man carefully.

He clenched his wife's hands in his own. "I need you to forgive me taking this out on you, love. I've not been the best person to live with this year, not since I lost my job. If I could rewind the last six months, I would."

Grace withdrew one of her hands and placed it on his

cheek. "I know. Life has been rough for all of us this year. But you've got a new job now and…"

"I have. I'm going to make it up to you, I promise."

Sam listened to the couple and couldn't help wondering if Grace was going to be gullible enough to believe what her husband was saying. Sam's own husband had struck out when money problems had blighted their lives. She shuddered as if someone had walked over her grave. She'd never fully understood that saying, not when the person who was shuddering was still alive, unlike her husband, who had taken his own sorry life and gone out in a blaze of glory.

"We'll see," Grace said, her voice emotional as tears welled up.

Sam stood. "We're going to leave you to it." She handed Grace one of her cards and smiled. "I'm at the end of a phone if you should ever need me. And if any information comes your way during the day, give me a call."

Grace took the card and showed them to the front door. Sam was dying to whisper a word of caution about her husband but thought better of it. It was never a good idea to interfere in someone's marriage, no matter how dicey you perceived it to be.

"Thank you for coming today, forcing us to deal with the issue."

"Hopefully it'll help you to get to grips quicker with what's happened. Sometimes it's not always the right thing to postpone the inevitable."

"I know. Can you tell me what the next step is?"

"The pathologist will be in touch with you once he's completed the post-mortem. You'll be given the opportunity to say farewell to your son before the funeral director gets involved. You might want to start thinking about that side of things in the next day or two."

"Oh gosh, I hadn't even thought about that. Do we have to foot the bill for the funeral? Or is that a daft question?"

"There are no silly questions at a time like this. Unfortunately, yes. They'll be able to give you guidance about possibly getting some of the costs covered, if you're eligible. I'm sorry, I'm not really up to date on that side of things. I suppose it depends if you're on benefits or not."

"Okay, I'll have a word with a few of the funeral directors. Are they around the same price?"

"I think they'll vary but I'm sure they'll still be competitively priced. Don't put too much pressure on yourself to get it all sorted today."

"Thank you, I'll take your advice on board. I know it's going to hit me again as soon as I close the door."

Let's hope that's all that hits you. "Take care, Grace. Don't forget, you've got my number if you need to run anything past me."

"I'll put your card away safely. Good luck with the investigation. I hope you find the person who has robbed us of our son, soon."

Sam held her crossed fingers up and smiled.

Grace closed the door, and Sam and Bob wandered back to the car.

"Let's hope he doesn't lay a hand on her now that we've left them to it," Bob said.

"I thought the same. She's a nice lady. I'm not sure about him, thought he was saying what he wanted us to hear most of the time."

"Yeah, his apology didn't sound sincere at all."

They travelled back to the station. During the journey, Sam was reflective throughout, and Bob picked up on it once they were out of the car.

"I hope you're not going to regret giving out yet another business card."

"Time will tell. The truth is, I wouldn't care if she did get in touch with me."

"Here we go again," he grumbled.

"Shut up. You're a miserable sod."

"Thanks. I'll add that to all the other names you've called me over the years."

She laughed. "Seriously, how are you holding up today, in light of what has come to our attention?"

"I'm taking it all in. Fuming that Lowther is adamant she hasn't got a problem at the school."

"We need to bide our time, Bob. Get all our facts together before we tackle her again on the subject. Dare I ask how it went at home last night? Did you get a chance to speak with Milly?"

"I tried. I had a word with Abigail, she's strong-willed as you know, keeps telling me to back off, let Milly come to us with her problems, but she's not hearing what we're coming up against, is she? And when I sit her down in the evening and try to explain what's going on, she doesn't want to know."

"That must be so frustrating for you. If there's anything I can do, all you have to do is ask."

"Thanks. I'm willing to sit on things for now, but after dealing with yet another victim from the same school this morning, it's going to be hard not to say anything when I get home tonight."

CHAPTER 7

Bob travelled home at just after six that evening. During the day he'd been through a gamut of emotions, worked himself into a tizzy, as Sam had called it, but thankfully seen the light at the end of the tunnel and emerged out the other side reasonably unscathed. But that was nothing compared to what he anticipated lay ahead of him when he stepped through the door to his home in a few minutes.

He turned the music up, doing his best to drown out the thoughts rattling around in his mind.

Bob drew into the driveway and switched off the engine. He didn't get out right away. Instead, he paused to practise a deep-breathing exercise Sam had taught him.

Minutes later, he was calm enough to enter the house. Abigail was in the kitchen, preparing the evening meal. He swooped in for a quick kiss and a cuddle. She offered up her cheek and wriggled out of his grasp.

"I'm busy. Can you lay the table for me? I called Milly about five minutes ago, but she hasn't come down for dinner yet."

"I'll go and check on her. How has she been today?"

"Quiet. I was in here, preparing the veg. She poked her head in to tell me she was home and then disappeared before I could ask if she'd had a good day at school."

Not what I want to hear. "I'll be right back."

"I need the table laid. Dinner will be ready to eat in less than five minutes. If the table isn't laid, we'll have to eat with our fingers."

"Don't fret. I won't be long, I promise."

He left Abigail taking her mood out on the saucepans on the stove. The banging noise followed him up the stairs. He paused outside Milly's bedroom, his ear against the door. He knocked. "Milly, can I come in?"

"I'm just changing, I'll be down in a sec, Dad."

"Slip your dressing gown on, I need to see you before we go downstairs."

"I said I won't be long. Please don't put pressure on me."

"I'm not. That's the last thing I want to do. Let me in, please?"

Milly yanked the door open. "What's wrong? Why can't I have any privacy around here?"

"Hey, it's all good, sweetheart. I was concerned about you and wanted to check you were all right. How did school go today?"

"Do we have to do this now? Mum sounds wound up down there. I think we should join her, don't you?"

"You win. Neither of us needs to get on the wrong side of your mother, do we?" Bob laughed, but Milly shrugged, not a glimmer of a smile in sight, which broke his heart. "Can we have a chat after dinner? It's important."

"Is it to do with my future? I told you last week, I'm not sure what I want to do yet. No doubt you'll be eager for me to sign up to the Force. To be honest with you, I'm not sure I have that in me, Dad."

"I wouldn't dream of trying to persuade you to sign up. I hope you've got a better career in mind than being a police officer. You're a lot brighter than me. You have a vast array of careers open to you, love. Still, you've got plenty of time ahead of you in which to decide where your future lies."

"Dinner's on the table, come and get it or it goes in the bin," Abigail called amidst more pot banging in the kitchen.

"We'd better get down there. I'm starving, I'd rather eat off a plate than scrabble around for scraps in the bin later, wouldn't you?"

Milly shrugged again. "I suppose so, although I haven't got much appetite at the moment."

He nudged her. "Don't let your mother hear you say that. Eat what you can, all right?"

She smiled and headed down the stairs in front of him. He watched the way she carried herself. Her shoulders appeared to have the weight of the world on them, and that hurt him, emotionally. Until a few months ago, Milly had wanted to spend all her spare time with either Abigail or him, mostly with her mother, which he'd accepted. However, in the last couple of months, that determination to be with them had all but diminished, and he struggled to put a finger on what was behind the change.

"Well, it's about time." Abigail said, her anger prominent for both to see. "I laid the table as well as cooked your meal. You two really need to start pulling your weight around here. It's rude and unacceptable to put the onus on me to do everything, got that?"

"Yes, dear," Bob said sincerely. He pulled out a chair for Abigail.

She glared at him and sat.

Milly sat next to her mother. "It looks delicious, Mum."

"And smells even better," Bob added.

They all tucked into the lasagne and salad Abigail had

spent hours preparing. Bob was the first to finish. He sipped at his orange juice and watched Milly push what was left of her meal around the plate.

"What's the matter with your food, Milly?" Abigail asked.

"Nothing, Mum, it's delicious, I'm just not hungry. Sorry."

"I don't know what's got into you lately, my girl. Half the time you're in a world of your own and the rest of the time you haven't got two words to say to us. I make no apologies for starting this conversation at the dinner table. It's about time you told us what's going on in that head of yours and why you always seem to be in a mood lately."

"I'm not," Milly muttered, her focus remaining on her plate. She put her knife and fork down and pushed back her chair.

Abigail slapped her hand over her daughter's and squeezed it. "You're not going anywhere, young lady. We're going to thrash this out, the three of us. No one is moving until I say so and we've resolved all the issues of what's going wrong with this family."

"We could be here for days." Bob chuckled, his aim to cut through the tension that had descended.

"I'm being deadly serious, Bob," she snarled. "We need to get to the truth here. I'm warning you, it either happens tonight or I go upstairs and pack a bag."

"What? Now you're just being ridiculous, love."

"Am I?" Abigail snapped.

Milly shoved her plate away and murmured something that Bob struggled to hear.

"What was that, Milly?" he asked.

"I said I don't care about anything any more. If Mum wants to go, there's little either you or I can do to stop her."

"At least I know where I stand." Abigail stood. "And you two can clear up the mess in here. I'm off out. I've arranged to meet a friend. Someone who appreciates my company.

Don't wait up for me, it could be a late one, if I come home at all."

"What? You can't walk out on us, Abigail."

She flounced out of the room and shouted, "Watch me. With me out of the way it might make you both rethink how much I do around here. Actually, I think I'll pack a bag and stay at Nichola's for a few days. That'll give us all the space we need to consider where this family is heading."

He attempted to go after Abigail, then realised it would be pointless and slumped back into his chair. "I think it would only make matters worse going after her. What do you think, Milly?"

Another shrug. "I'm not married, I don't know what the rules are. You're on your own, Dad."

"All of this could have been avoided if only you would open up to us, Mils."

She stared at him, her eyes widened. "Are you saying this is my fault?"

"Partially. We're worried about you, and it's causing added tension within our relationship."

Milly shook her head. "I've heard it all now." She stood and tucked her chair under the table. "I'll be in my room, you know, wallowing in self-pity like I usually do."

"What? No one has said that."

"You didn't have to. You're not the only one who has the ability to read between the lines."

"What about the washing-up?" he whined.

"You do it. It's not like you have to do it every night, Mum usually has to do everything."

"Hey, don't walk away from me, Milly, you're as much to blame about that as I am."

She stood in the doorway and asked, "How old am I, Dad?"

"Fifteen. What does that have to do with anything?"

"I'm the kid in this house. You two are the adults, chores should be shared equally, right?"

"Hey, kids play a part in the running of a household, too, and furthermore, Miss Jones, you're not too old for me to put you across my knee."

"Ah, but wouldn't you be breaking the law if you thrashed the life out of me these days?"

He grumbled, knowing how accurate her retort was.

What a day, and what an even worse evening, and now I'm lumbered with doing the crappy washing-up by myself, too. Still, with Abigail out of the way this evening, hopefully it will give me the chance to have a quiet word with Milly. Then again, she'll probably put the shutters down and choose to ignore me, as usual.

He got on with the washing-up with his mind still firmly on what had happened during the day. Ten minutes later and with a holdall in her hand, Abigail appeared in the doorway. "I'll ring you tomorrow. I need this time away, Bob. Don't try and contact me."

He turned and wiped his hands on a tea towel. "I take it there's no point in you hanging around, thrashing this out between us?"

"None whatsoever. Sorry, I need a break, not only from Milly but from everything, the house, me doing the lion's share of all the chores, something that's never appreciated by anyone else. The constant treading on eggshells to avoid an atmosphere around here. *Everything.*"

"So, you're just going to walk away from us, is that it? Do you have any intention of coming back, or is this finally it for us as a family?"

"Ask me that in a couple of days when I've sorted things out in my head."

"How long have you been planning this?"

"How dare you? I haven't been planning anything of the

sort. We all have a limit we need to reach before we take the appropriate action. I reached that limit tonight."

"Why, all because I didn't lay the table for you? I was upstairs, trying to get Milly to open up to me, to us, and now you're punishing me for that tiny indiscretion." He threw the tea towel on the side and glared at her.

She held his gaze for a few moments then turned her back on him.

"Walk away from me tonight and we're done," he said. "If you're not going to allow me to voice my opinion about what's going wrong with this family then what's the point in us staying together, being married?"

"Whatever," she called over her shoulder. Seconds later, the front door slammed.

He removed his phone from his pocket and texted her, *You're being unfair... just saying.*

She replied several minutes later, *I don't think I am. You need to live in my shoes for a day or two. Carry out the chores I do during the day. I work full-time as well, in case you've forgotten that crucial fact.*

I haven't, he typed back. *The ball is in your court. We'll await your decision.*

He stared at the phone, waited for a response to appear on his screen, but it never came. He switched on the kettle then turned it off again after realising he would need something stronger than just tea. He filled a glass with a two-inch shot of whisky and returned to his seat at the table to mull over how he was going to handle Milly. He decided the only way forward was to be honest and direct with her. After downing his drink, he pulled his shoulders back and ascended the stairs armed with a slice of Bakewell tart he found in the fridge. It was Milly's favourite, and he hoped it would break down the barrier between them.

Bob knocked on Milly's door and waited for her to invite

him in. It never came, so he knocked again. "Milly, I think we need to talk."

"I don't. Please, Dad, leave me alone. I'm tired and I've got loads of homework to do."

Enough was enough. He barged into the room to find her sitting on the bed, painting her toenails.

"Funny-looking homework. I brought you some cake but didn't bother with a drink, I know how fussy you are."

"Thanks, leave it on the cabinet, I'll have it in a minute. You're free to go now."

Bob shook his head and narrowed his eyes. "Don't even go there. Stop treating people in this house like they're your own personal skivvies, you hear me?"

She paused painting her toes and glared at him. "I've never treated either you or Mum as my skivvy. Why would you even think that?"

"I had to clean up the kitchen and do the dishes myself. That task was supposed to be a job for both of us."

"I'm sorry. I couldn't face it."

"That's tough, we all have chores to carry out in this life that we hate doing, we just need to knuckle down and do them unless we have a genuine reason for not doing them."

"I had homework to do." The colour rose in her cheeks.

"Pull the other one."

"It's the truth, I can't force you to believe me. I've finished one lot, my English Literature, and thought I'd paint my nails before I started on my Physics. We all need to give our brains a break now and again. This is my time. I always take a breather between subjects, that way I'm less likely to get them mixed up. It's how I was advised to do it by my form teacher years ago."

He raised an eyebrow as if querying what she'd said.

"It's true, ask Mrs Knight if you don't believe me. Christ,

now I'm sitting here, feeling like a criminal. Was that your intention?"

"Don't be so absurd. If you want to take this down the station, I'm not averse to that, just give me the nod and it could be arranged."

"Stop being an idiot, Dad. You wouldn't dare drag me down there, you'd only be causing yourself embarrassment."

"Don't tempt me. Everyone has problems with teenagers. I'm all for scaring the crap out of you guys if it will make you take a step back to think about the disruption you're causing to a family."

"I'm doing no such thing."

"You are, you simply don't realise it. Why else do you think your mother walked out on us tonight?"

"She said she needs space from both of us, so we're both to blame."

"No, it's officially down to you, dealing with shit you're not prepared to share with us. So come on, no more dancing around the issue, what's going on?"

Milly continued to paint her nails which only infuriated him further. He allowed her to finish the left foot but then removed the bottle and brush from her hands before she could start on the right one.

"No, you're not going to avoid me a moment longer. We're going to sit here, like adults, until you tell me what's bugging you. I have an inkling I know what it is, but I need you to come out and tell me."

"You might think you know, but I'm telling you straight there is nothing going on with me, Dad."

He heaved out a sigh of frustration. "Why are you intent on making this so difficult for me? For us? Just admit what's going on so we can all move on and your mother can come home, or was that the plan? To drive your mother out of the house?"

She held her head low. "Of course it wasn't. This isn't down to me, Dad."

"What isn't down to you?"

"The fact Mum has walked out on us. How do you know she hasn't got another fella on the go?"

"What a crass thing to suggest about your own mother, how dare you?"

"It's not at all. I've heard you at night in your bedroom, arguing lately. I've not heard any 'action' going on between you in ages. And yes, the walls are thinner than you think they are."

Shit! It was his turn to colour up. "All the arguments or heated discussions we've had have been about you and your problems."

Milly's gaze dropped to the carpet beside her.

"Sweetheart, I can't help you if you refuse to open up to me. We've never had problems between us in the past. This is tearing me apart. I feel useless, totally inadequate as a father."

He reached for her hand, and she allowed him to interlock fingers with hers.

"I'm sorry. I didn't mean to cause you so much pain. I've been trying to deal with the situation in my own way without involving you guys. Can you forgive me?"

"For what? What's there to forgive, for God's sake? Come on, love, we're halfway there now. You've admitted there's a problem, now all you have to do is tell me what it is so that we can get through it together, as a family."

"You said that you had an inkling what was wrong. You tell me and I'll say if you're right or not."

"Okay, but first you have to promise to give me all the facts afterwards. Deal?"

"If you're right, yes."

"I think this is to do with the crimes we've been dealing with this week. I had to go to the school, your school, and question your head about bullying issues. Are you being bullied, Mils?"

Silence and yet more silence followed. Bob allowed her time to consider what he'd asked her before he tried a second time.

"Milly, I'm not trying to pressure you into telling me, but your Mum and I are both desperately worried about you."

She inhaled and exhaled several times and even shuddered once or twice.

Rather than give up, Bob tried a different tack. "Mils, do you know the name Leo Burke?"

He studied her reaction carefully and even reached for her hand after he saw her balling her fists. She relented and slipped her hand into his. Her palm was sweaty.

"How do you know him?"

Her breathing came in short sharp bursts; her chest inflated and deflated swiftly. "I can't," she murmured.

He shuffled closer towards her on the bed. "Why, sweetie? Don't you trust me?"

She looked him in the eye, and her voice caught on a sob. "Of course I do, Dad."

He gathered her in his arms and rubbed his hand up and down her back. "I hate to see you like this. I don't know what to do to help you. Please let me in. Confide in me, it needn't go any further, love. I need to know what, if anything, or should I say who, has affected your life in such a devastating way. Will you tell me what's bothering you? How do you know Burke?"

"He's a pupil at my school. What's he done?"

"I'm sorry to have to tell you he's dead, love."

She pulled away from him and, wide-eyed, repeated what he said. "He's dead? How?"

"Someone murdered him last night. I have to add what I'm confiding in you must remain between us. You can't go to school tomorrow and share the information with your friends."

"I promise. I can't believe he's dead."

"How do you know him? I was watching your reaction, and it was what I would call telling."

She shook her head and said, "I can't. Please, don't force me to tell you."

"Force you? I would never force you to do anything. What have I done to you that is making you so anxious, putting doubt in your mind?"

"Doubt in my mind? About what?"

"Trusting me. We used to be best pals. You always loved spending time with either me or your mother, and now, you can't bear to be near us. We need to know why. Have we failed you, let you down in some way?"

"No, Dad. It's nothing like that. I'm sorry, I thought shutting myself away would be the answer, and all it has done was raise your suspicions about me."

"I'm going to ask you one last time... are you being bullied?"

Another spell of silence followed, then fresh tears splashed onto her cheeks when she nodded. "Yes," she whispered the one word he'd been dreading hearing.

He pulled her into his arms again to hide his own tears. "Why couldn't you come to us? Why, love? No one needs to deal with this, and especially not alone, like you have."

She leaned back and kissed his cheek. "I know that now, but I didn't at the time. I didn't want you to feel sorry for me."

"Sorry for you? It's not a case of that, sweetheart. These morons need to be stopped before they ruin someone's life, not that they haven't done that already. These types of situations tend to gather momentum. The more powerful the bullies think they are the worse their crimes become, as in this case, they've possibly taken a life. Does that make sense?"

"Yes but... you've got this all wrong." Milly shook her head. "It doesn't matter."

"It damn well does matter, if I'm missing something vital you need to tell me."

She picked at the hem of her skirt. "Jesus, this is so hard… only because I know where it is going to lead to."

"What will? Come on, sweetheart, you've been brave enough to come this far, you might as well tell me everything now."

Milly closed her eyes, and her breathing became erratic once more. He waited for a few moments before he felt the need to prompt her again.

Bob squeezed her hands. "Mils, tell me what's going on, please?"

She shook her head several times, and the tears fell.

He was at a loss as to what he should do next to coax the information out of her. "Milly, we can put a stop to this, if only you will trust me."

"There's a gang of them. How do you stop a gang, Dad?"

"Of girls or boys?"

"Boys."

"Does the head know? Tell me, is she aware there's a problem with bullying at her school? Because she denied it when I visited her this week."

She shrugged. "I'm not sure, maybe she is, maybe she isn't. She never raises the subject in assembly or at any other time."

"Why do you think that is? Sorry for asking, putting you in this position, as if you're likely to know. Is it a major issue at the school?"

She nodded.

"There are five of them. They terrorise people in the hallways but usually go after the other students on their way home, when they are off the school premises."

"How long has this been going on?"

"Months. I can't tell you exactly."

She glanced away and was unable to maintain eye contact with him. Instinct was telling him that she was holding something back, but what?

"Is there anything else you can tell me, love?"

She gulped noisily and trained all her focus on the door behind him.

"Milly? Anything you tell me will remain between you and me, I promise."

She shook her head. "Don't lie to me. I know as soon as I reveal the truth you'll be on the phone to the station, so don't give me that bullshit, Dad. Stop treating me like an idiot."

He laughed. "You know me so well. But if you're holding back something important…"

She sucked in a large breath and mumbled, "He was one of them."

Bob's head shot back. He could feel his double chin emerge and returned his head back in its normal position. "Who was, Burke? Is that what you're telling me?"

"Yes. He's been making our lives miserable for months… he and his gang."

"Can you give me the names of the other gang members?"

"I can't, Dad, please don't make me do that. I've told you far more than I wanted to tell you as it is."

"Will I be able to find out who the others are by asking around at the school?"

"I think so. I apologise if you think I'm letting you down by not telling you."

"I don't. I'm grateful for you telling me the truth here tonight. If this gang ever approaches you again, I want you to ring me right away and I'll come down and sort them out."

She smiled and touched her hand against his cheek. "My hero."

He laughed and wrapped his arms around her. They shared a hug, the kind they used to share up until a few months ago.

"I love you. I'm sorry all this shit has spoilt our relationship. I hope you and Mum will be able to forgive me, eventually."

"You don't need to seek our forgiveness, we will always love you, Milly, through good times and bad, and I assure you, throughout life there will be a mixture of both that will test us."

"Thanks, Dad. Do you think Mum will come home now, or do you think she's gone for good this time?"

"I hope not, sweetie. Let's give it a day for her to calm down. I'll give her a call after work tomorrow, to see where the land lies, and we'll take it from there. Now, do you fancy a bowl of salted caramel ice cream?"

"I'd love one. Can we snuggle up and watch a movie together, like the old days?"

"I'm sure that could be arranged."

They hugged once more, and then Milly raced him to the door and down the stairs. It felt good to have his daughter back, if only briefly, before the next trauma hits their lives.

CHAPTER 8

"Morning, ma'am, I know this isn't what you want to hear when you come in first thing in the morning but..." Nick said.

Sam rolled her eyes and said, "Let's have it, you might as well spoil my day before it's really had a chance to get going."

"I can't apologise enough. There was an attack last night on another boy."

"Jesus, how serious is it?"

"Bad enough. He's in hospital with a knife wound. Luckily the perpetrator missed all the vital organs."

"Okay, we'll head over there as soon as Bob gets in."

"Talking about me again, are you?" Bob shouted from the main door.

Sam groaned and turned to face him. "Trust you to come in on the end of a conversation and get the wrong end of the stick."

"What's going on? Why the serious faces?"

"Nick's just informed me there's been an attack on another lad. I've yet to hear the rest of the details."

Nick passed her a sheet of paper. On it was the mother's address.

"No father on the scene?" Sam asked.

"No, he died a few years ago. The lad is fifteen, same age as the previous victim."

"Thanks, Nick. Will you let the team know that we're on our way to the hospital? And if the mother isn't there, we'll drop over and see her while we're out, too."

"Leave it with me, ma'am. Good luck."

"Thanks."

Sam and Bob left the station, and she noticed her partner was somewhat subdued.

"Everything all right, Bob?"

"Not really. Abigail walked out on me last night."

She stopped and clawed at his arm to prevent him from walking on. "She what? Why?"

"I'll tell you en route. Let's just say arriving this morning to this news hasn't done me any favours."

"I'm not with you, what's that supposed to mean?"

"In the car," he repeated.

She continued towards her vehicle, her mind thinking all sorts, none of them pleasant.

"Right, now tell me, I can't wait a moment longer."

He sighed and relayed the events that had led up to Abigail walking out on him and Milly. Halfway through the conversation, Sam started the engine and got on the road.

"But that's life, isn't it? Living with a teenager? There's always going to be days where hormones are at their worst, isn't there?"

"I haven't told you the best bit yet."

"Heck, there's more?"

"Hold on to your hat for this one… after Abigail left, I couldn't hack it any more. I went to see Milly in her room. She tried to avoid speaking to me, but I firmly put my foot down. She finally admitted what has been wrong with her the last few months."

He paused.

Sam delayed her response, hoping he would start speaking again. Eventually, she had to ask, "And? What did she say?"

"She confessed that it was down to bullying. Told me there was a gang of five who were terrorising the school."

"I don't suppose you coaxed the names out of her, did you?"

"One of them, yes."

Another pause.

"Come on, Bob, you can be so infuriating at times. Just tell me."

"The name was Leo Burke."

Sam slammed on the brakes. The car behind almost ran into the back of her. The driver blasted his horn continuously until she got out of the car and apologised. He gesticulated for her to get a move on. She drove off, dumbfounded, and drew into a lay-by just up the road.

"Say that again?"

"Judging by your reaction, I think you heard me the first time."

"I did but I can't quite believe what I heard. Leo Burke was a bully? What does this mean? That someone turned on him? Another member of the gang perhaps?"

"More than likely. If they had a disagreement about something. Maybe he wanted to leave the gang and the leader decided to punish him."

"Shit! There are so many scenarios playing out in my mind right now. This is unbelievable. Now we've got another lad lying in a hospital bed, just like Ben Cox. None of this is making any sense."

"That's the nature of the beast, isn't it? An investigation

rarely runs smoothly. Maybe we can kill two birds with one stone and visit Ben while we're there."

"What's behind that notion? That he might be able to give us more names?"

"Or at least tell us what happened to him."

"We're going to have to be cautious with him, in case he's not feeling up to speaking with us yet."

"What tangled webs we weave, eh?"

"You could say that."

LUCKILY FOR THEM, the victim they had come to visit happened to be on the same ward as Ben. The nurse recognised Sam and Bob as soon as she saw them.

"Back so soon?" she said.

"Actually, we've come to see another boy, Aiden Haley, he was brought in last night. So, if it's possible, we'd like to have a word with him and Ben, if they're up to it?"

"Ben is still pretty much the same. His brother has been a godsend, keeping his spirits up, but he's still not said much really. The other boy keeps drifting in and out of consciousness. His mother is with him. Perhaps you can chat with her first, I doubt if Aiden will be up to speaking with you at this time."

"Thanks, that might be the best option for us."

"I'll take you to them."

Sam and Bob followed the nurse who stopped at the first bed on the right.

"One quick question, has Ben's aunt visited him?" Sam asked.

"Not while I've been on duty. Only his brother. He arrives after school kicks out and stays here for around three to four hours. He's an absolute gem of a boy. So polite, and we never have any problems with him. We generally have a whip-round to buy him a sandwich and a drink while he's here."

"That's kind of you. Thank you for looking out for him."

She drew back the curtain slightly and announced their arrival to a brunette sitting by her son's bed.

"Do I have to talk to you now? My son is in a bad way. I'm not sure I can tell you anything, anyway."

"The sooner we speak with you the better, Mrs Haley," Sam replied with a smile.

"In the corridor then, not here."

"Suits us."

The nurse led the way back to her station, and then Mrs Haley accompanied Sam and Bob off the ward.

Mrs Haley sat in one of the chairs, clearly exhausted, and put her head in her hands. "It's been a long night."

"Are you up to telling us how this happened? No pressure."

"I was at a friend's house, she's just lost her husband, you see. I returned home at about nine, and Aiden wasn't there. I began to get worried. I went out searching for him; he usually hangs around the park after school, riding his bike. When I got there it was empty. I was about to leave when I saw something glimmer in the distance, it must have been from the streetlight close by. I walked towards the area to take a look and that's when I realised Aiden's bike was lying behind the bushes, but the handlebars were poking out and the light was catching on them."

She paused, and her bottom lip quivered.

Sam sat beside her and covered Mrs Haley's hand with hers. "It's okay. In your own time."

"I cried out for help, but no one came. He was lying there, behind the bushes, his eyes closed. I took out my phone, put the torch on and almost dropped it. There was blood all over his white T-shirt. I couldn't tell how much he had lost because he was lying on the soil. I rang for an ambulance right away, and the police attended as well. They searched the area while we waited for the ambulance to arrive; they didn't see anyone hanging around. I drove here, to the hospital, and haven't left."

"And how is your son? What's the prognosis?"

"They think he's going to be all right. Although it seemed bad at the time, the consultant said Aiden was lucky the knife didn't hit any of his major organs or it might have been fatal."

"That's a relief. Has Aiden woken up at all?"

"He's opened his eyes a couple of times, tried to speak but gave up. He hasn't even had the energy to lift his head, let alone talk. I know the doctor keeps telling me he's going to be all right, but I have my doubts, he's so weak. He's usually a bright boy, full of mischief, always trying to play practical jokes on me when I least expect it. To see him like this is… killing me. Oh God, I wish my husband was here, he'd know what to do. Unfortunately, I lost him to cancer a few years ago, a hardworking man cut down in his prime. We were at the stage of starting to look forward to our future together, once the kids were off our hands."

"How many do you have?"

"Aiden obviously, plus he has an older sister. She spent part of the night here with me. I told her to go home and get some rest at eight this morning. She's five months pregnant, expecting her first child. We were all looking forward to welcoming the new baby, even Aiden."

"Please, you need to remain positive."

"I'm trying. It's not the easiest thing to do, not when I see how frail he is."

"Can I ask you if your son has discussed being bullied at school?"

She frowned. "No, he's never mentioned it. Why do you ask? So, you think another pupil did this to him?"

"It's possible. We're investigating several cases of this nature this week. Does your son know Ben Cox?"

"I don't know, and I won't be able to ask him until he wakes up and is able to speak to me."

"What about Dean Grady, Mark Powell, or Leo Burke, do any of those names ring a bell?"

"Yes, Leo. He spends a lot of time with a Leo. I couldn't tell you his surname, though, I'm sorry."

"That's okay. Do they spend time at the park together, on their bikes?"

Mrs Haley smiled. "Yes, I've met him a couple of times, he seems a nice enough lad. Why do you ask? Have they been bullied as well, is that what you're getting at?"

"We're still investigating the possibility."

"Goodness me. I didn't realise the school had a problem. We only moved to the area three years ago. I can't believe this is the first I'm hearing about it now. Are the school co-operating with you?"

Sam held her hand up and waved it from side to side. "Not really. We're going over there now to see what the head has to say."

"Good. You hear about too many incidences like this where the heads don't care. It seems they're all too keen to brush the problem under the carpet. I know the Soaps do their best to highlight the fact that bullying is still rife in schools but, nothing seems to be done about it by the authorities. Years ago, around five, I think, my friend withdrew her child from school because there was an issue with bullying, but the teachers and the head didn't want to know. Her daughter suffered health wise, she became very withdrawn. My friend finally said enough was enough, gave up her job and began home-schooling her child herself."

"That's amazing. She's to be admired although, saying that, not every parent is in a position to do that, whether it proves to be for the greater good for the child or not should also be a consideration. Do you happen to know the name of the other boys your son hangs around with at school?"

Mrs Haley chewed on her lip. "I can't think, what with what's going on with my son. I'm sorry. If you hadn't mentioned Leo's name I wouldn't have been able to have offered it up myself."

"Don't worry, we'll see if someone at the school can help us. We're going to let you get back to your son now. Take care, and thanks again for speaking with us."

"Hopefully what I've told you will help your investigation. Sorry it wasn't much."

"Don't worry."

She smiled and returned to the ward.

"Miracle of miracles, you didn't give her a card."

Sam swiped at him. "Easily remedied." And she walked back onto the ward. "It's only me again. I forgot to give you one of my cards."

Mrs Haley smiled and accepted it. "Thank you."

Sam pulled the curtain closed again and joined Bob who was lingering outside the area where Ben was. She drew back the curtain. Ben stared back at her and cowered in his bed.

"Hey, Ben, it's only me, Sam Cobbs. We met the other day, do you remember?"

His brow wrinkled, and after a few seconds, he nodded. "Yes, I do. Sorry, I've not been good since the attack."

"Is anyone here with you?"

"No, Josh is at school, and I'm not sure where my aunt is."

"Are you up to talking with us?"

"I think so. I'm not too tired, but that could change quickly."

Sam stepped inside, invited Bob to join them, and then drew the curtain closed behind them. There was only one chair. Bob took that, and Sam sat on the edge of the bed near Ben's feet, wary of overcrowding him too much.

"First of all, how are you feeling?"

"I'm okay, mostly. My head still hurts every so often."

"Are they still sending you for the scans?"

"Yes."

"Have they told you when they're going to release you?"

"No. I think I'd rather stay in hospital for a few days… umm, to make sure I'm fully recovered rather than go back to my aunt's," he added quickly, maybe a little too quickly for Sam's liking.

"Is everything all right at home with Josh and your aunt?"

His gaze dropped to his legs, and it took him a while to answer. "Yes, I think so. We're grateful for her letting us stay there."

"Yes, it was a very kind gesture of her to take you and your brother on, especially at such short notice."

He nodded but didn't look Sam in the eye which left her wondering if anything serious had happened between Josh and his aunt. "Are you up to talking about what happened to you at the park?"

"Umm… I suppose so, not that I can remember much, not really. I'd left the school gates. I got bored of hanging around, waiting for Josh, he'd been gone a while. I decided to walk home. I went through the park. I didn't get far when the gang appeared. They circled me on their bikes. I didn't see their faces, they had their caps on, pulled down low. Josh knows them, though, or thinks he does. They're older boys. They were vile. They were being nasty about my dad, saying he was a coward for… taking his own life. Told me that he couldn't stand the thought of being around me and Josh any more after Mum dying. Maybe… thinking about it now, they were telling the truth, but at the time I didn't want to believe it was true."

"You mustn't think that, love. I'm sure your father loved the bones of you and Josh. He was still grieving the loss of your mother. Grief can be so hard to deal with for some folks, but that has no reflection on how he felt about you and Josh. He left you a note to say how much he loved you both. I haven't mentioned that before and I haven't got the note with me. When you're stronger, I promise I will show it to you."

"He did? Can you tell me what it said? I knew Dad wouldn't leave us... not without saying goodbye."

"I can't tell you word for word, but he said how much he loved you and how much he missed your mother. It was a heartfelt message to you both."

He began sobbing, and Sam could have kicked herself for bringing up the letter. "Hey, I didn't mean to upset you. It's a good thing, it proves that your father was thinking about you and Josh right up to the end."

He shook his head, and his face creased up. "If he'd thought anything of us, he'd still be here today. We miss him, I miss him. I'm lost without him. I wouldn't be in hospital with all these injuries if he hadn't... killed himself. What type of father does that? Leaves his kids to survive in a wicked world like this?"

Sam reached for his hand. He surprised her by allowing her to comfort him. "I know this is hard to take in, who knows what goes on in someone's head before they take their own life? But I'm sure, that in his heart, he felt he was doing the right thing for both of you."

"But how? We've got nothing and we're living with... a woman we hardly know. How is that right? We had a home we loved, okay, it would have been full of memories for Dad, for us, but he could have moved if it was too much for him. But no... he chose... I hate to admit it, but those boys were right, the coward's way out."

"No, I refuse to allow you to believe that. Your father

wasn't thinking straight when he did what he did. I can't emphasise that enough."

"Josh and I have spoken about it; we both feel the same way. If Dad was to walk in here now, I'm not sure I would ever be able to forgive him for deserting us the way he did. One minute he was at home cooking our dinner and giving us breakfast in the morning, and the next he... well, you know what he did. What type of man does that? I'm sorry if I keep repeating myself, but it's hard for me to understand how a parent can leave their kids."

"I know. I think you're too young to fully comprehend."

"I'm not. I understand exactly, I just don't get it. How could he leave us, without a parent to guide us through life? He was selfish. I've been lying here going over things, and that's what I've come up with, it was a super selfish act."

Tears misted Sam's eyes. While she agreed with his observation, she was determined to steer him in another direction, knowing that the truth would continue to eat away at him for years, if not for the rest of his life. "You mustn't think that, Ben, your father did what he did out of desperation. The grief was all-consuming for him."

"We were all grieving. Don't you think we missed our mother as much as he did? We did, I can assure you, and who is left picking up the pieces? Me and my brother, two teenage boys living in a world that is so much harder to live in these days. I could go over and over it for hours and get nowhere. There's no point in doing that, not now he's gone. If only he'd had the balls to talk things over with us. He was a good actor, hid his true feelings a lot of the time; both Josh and I have said the same thing. As far as we knew Dad was all right. That's what we're having trouble dealing with."

Sam squeezed his hand. He withdrew it from her grasp.

"Maybe it's better for you not to think too much about it," she said. "I know that will be hard, but look at it this way, you can't turn back the clock, you and Josh both need to move forward with your lives."

"That's easy for you to say. We've been kicked out of our home and forced to live with a woman we hardly know."

"Has your aunt been treating you well?"

He fell silent again. Raising Sam's suspicions about whether moving the boys in with the aunt had been the right option for them after all. She'd need to ring Georgina, run all of this past her before the day was out. She groaned inwardly at her to-do list, growing ever longer.

"Okay, is there anything else you can tell us about the attack? Did any of the boys use each other's name?"

He paused to mull over her question. "I think I heard the name Marco, but I can't be sure. You'll have to ask Josh; he knows the gang."

"We'll do that. Is there anything else we can get you before we go? A drink or something to eat from the shop?"

"No, Josh has been really good, and the nurses have, too. They look after me well, make a fuss over me. I'm so grateful to them for being so kind to me."

"We all want the best for you and your brother, Ben. It's a reminder that you're not alone, or it should be."

"I know. Thank you."

She waved and left the cubicle with Bob.

"I feel so sorry for that kid," he said. "Being abandoned by his father only to get beaten up by those effing thugs, is it any wonder he's down in the dumps?"

"Hard to comprehend a kid of that age having to contend with what he's been through the last six months. I think he'll come through it okay, with Josh by his side."

"Yeah, I don't think the same thing can be said about the aunt though, can it? What are you going to do about her?"

"Remind me to ring Social Services after we've visited the school, that's next on our agenda."

"Good luck with that one. I bet you don't get anything out of the head. I didn't the other day."

Sam winked and grinned at him. "We'll see. I might give Georgina a call en route. Fancy driving?"

"I'm up for it."

SAM ENDED the call with Georgina with a knot in her stomach. She had laid out all the facts, and Georgina had made all the right noises during the conversation, but Sam had her doubts if it was going to make a blind bit of difference. As far as she was concerned, they had placed the children with a family member, job done. She got the impression that Georgina was being stifled at her end, as if she was afraid of saying what she truly thought in front of her colleagues, who might have been lurking nearby.

Now all they had to do was tackle Mrs Lowther and enforce upon her the fact that there was a bullying problem at her school whether she wanted to accept there was, or not. Sam had the facts to prove it.

The receptionist welcomed them with a cautious smile and agreed to ring Mrs Lowther to ask if she had time to see them. The answer was yes. The receptionist then showed them down the corridor towards the head's office. Several teenagers came towards them, one of them Sam thought she recognised as Bob's daughter. She turned to face him. He was waving at Milly, but she totally blanked him.

"Don't get upset, she's with her friends, she's probably too embarrassed to acknowledge you."

"I'm okay, don't worry about me. I was a teenager once as well, you know. I would have been mortified if one of my parents showed up on official business at the school."

Sam smiled. "That's the spirit. Hey, at least she's got friends."

He laughed. "That's true. I was a bit of a loner during my school days."

"Aww… were you? I can't imagine that."

The receptionist knocked on the head's door, and they entered the room. Mrs Lowther shuffled the papers on her desk and, for a few moments, avoided eye contact with them.

"Inspector, Sergeant, what can I do for you on this dull, windy day?"

"Unfortunately, we have reason to believe that despite you telling my partner otherwise, you do indeed have a problem with bullying at this school."

"Preposterous. I repeat, we have no such thing."

"I beg to differ. During the investigation we have carried out this week, we have put a huge dent in your assertion."

Mrs Lowther raised an eyebrow and linked her fingers together. "What is this proof you keep talking about?"

"We've just come from the hospital where we visited two boys. One was Ben Cox, the boy we had to break the sad news to about his father, in this very office."

"I remember. Please refrain from treating me like an idiot, Inspector."

Sam ploughed on. "The second boy, who we believe is also a pupil at this school, is Aiden Haley."

Mrs Lowther nodded. "I know the lad. Do you mind telling me how he ended up in hospital?"

"He was stabbed, luckily not too seriously, but badly enough to warrant a stay in hospital."

"I'm sorry to hear that. Has he given you any indication of who attacked him?"

"No, he was sleeping when we got there. But there's more. This week, another boy, Leo Burke, was fatally wounded, also in a knife attack."

"Yes, I'm aware. I was informed by his parents. A dreadful incident."

"And you still don't believe there's an issue here?"

Mrs Lowther opened her mouth to speak, but Sam raised a hand to silence her.

"Before you answer that, we've also been in touch with some other parents this week, regarding attacks that happened a few months ago. Both their sons, Dean Grady and Mark Powell, were also attacked by a gang of thugs from this school."

"Now wait just a minute, you can't go around making bizarre accusations like that. I've spoken to both those boys, at length may I add, and not once have they opened up to me and told me they were attacked by pupils from this school. Therefore, I believe you're barking up the wrong tree, Inspector."

"Far from it, Mrs Lowther. The parents have told us otherwise, and we intend to do something about it. Then, there's the issue of Sergeant Jones' own daughter admitting that she has been bullied on school premises."

Bob nodded. "It's true. She finally broke down and admitted it to me."

"Why hasn't she come to me?"

"Maybe the pupils are too scared to approach you, Mrs Lowther," Sam suggested.

"What? Don't be absurd. I've never heard anything so ridiculous in my twenty years of teaching, four of which have been as headmistress at this school."

"Whether you choose to believe it or not, it's the truth, Mrs Lowther. Here's another surprising turn of events. Milly told her father, when pushed for a name, that Leo Burke, the boy who sadly died this week, hadn't been bullied, he was actually one of the bullies."

She shook her head. "What utter nonsense. Leo was a good pupil at this school. I think your daughter is making this up, Sergeant."

"She's not," Bob said with conviction. "She was terrified to tell me, afraid of what the repercussions might be. Why would she lie about something like this?"

"I don't know, you tell me," Lowther retorted snootily.

Sam sensed things were getting heated between Bob and Lowther.

"What we need to ask is whether you're prepared to work with us to overcome this issue or if we're going to have to take things into our own hands."

"I have always worked with the police in the past, I have no objection about doing that this time around."

"Thank you. Perhaps you can start by telling us who Leo Burke hung around with?"

"I meant, at my convenience. Today I have back-to-back meetings with parents, and no, that's not me skirting around the issues that you've raised here today. You're going to have to excuse me, the first meeting is due to start in fifteen minutes and I still have a few bits and pieces I need to do before it begins."

Sam inclined her head. "Perhaps you can tell me when you'll be able to squeeze us into your busy schedule then?"

"I believe I have a spare half an hour available tomorrow afternoon."

"It's not ideal. I truly believe this problem needs to be taken seriously and I can't help thinking that you're giving us the brush-off, Mrs Lowther."

"I'm doing no such thing. I'm a very busy person, trying to run a school with three hundred and fifty pupils. You really can't expect me to drop everything the minute you set foot inside my school. I bent over backwards to accommodate you the other day, sorting out the Cox boys, so I don't think you can sit there and accuse me of being unreasonable, do you?"

Sam had to agree, she had a point. "I can't deny I'm disappointed that we can't get things sorted today, particularly as I regard this as an urgent matter."

"I also have an afternoon full of what the parents I have scheduled to meet with today would class as urgent matters."

"These meetings, tell me, would you regard them as life-or-death meetings?"

Mrs Lowther scowled at Sam. "No, but if I start letting parents down who have taken time off work to come here today, it wouldn't be long before I received a bad reputation for being unreliable. So, as you can appreciate, I find myself in a no-win situation."

"And where does that leave us? What about your deputy head, is he or she available to chat with us?"

"No, Mrs Silver is away in Portugal, visiting her parents at present."

"A senior teacher perhaps? You must have one of them in a school this size, surely?"

"We do. I can call Mr Fitzpatrick, ask him if he can fit you in."

"Thank you, that would be better than us leaving here empty-handed today and feeling like we've been an inconvenience to you."

"I'm sorry if that's how it has come across, it wasn't my intention." She picked up the phone and pressed a number. "Charles, are you busy…? Can you spare me ten minutes of your valuable time…? Yes, it's important… I need you to deal with the police for me…I'll expect to see you soon." She ended the call and smiled awkwardly. "He's on his way."

"Thank you. Shall we wait in the corridor for him?"

"Yes, I think Mr and Mrs Knorr will be here shortly and I still have to locate their son's file before the meeting takes place."

"We appreciate your time today. We'll be in touch soon."

Mrs Lowther dismissed them with a curt nod, and they

left the office. The two chairs immediately outside were occupied by a man and woman, clutching hands, who appeared to be gravely concerned about what lay ahead of them. Sam was tempted to strike up a conversation with the couple, but the opportunity was stripped from her when Mrs Lowther opened her office door again and summoned Mr and Mrs Knorr.

The couple released each other's hand and entered the head's office.

"What do you think that was all about?" Bob whispered in her ear as they watched a man in a dark suit walk towards them.

"I don't know. I can hazard a guess, though. I think there's a huge cover-up going on around here and it's pissing me off."

"I totally agree with you. Something is beginning to reek of week-old fish."

The man stopped a few feet in front of them. "Hello, I'm Charles Fitzpatrick. You wanted to see me?"

Sam and Bob produced their warrant cards, and Sam introduced herself to Fitzpatrick, who now seemed puzzled to be meeting with them.

"No, actually, what we requested was to have a meeting with Mrs Lowther, but she has other ideas and has palmed us off onto you."

"Oh, I see. I'm sorry to hear that. We'd better make the best of the situation then. Would you like to come back to my office, or do you want to speak to me here?"

"Your office will be fine."

The three of them walked past another group of pupils in the corridor, on their way somewhere.

"Chop, chop, boys, you'll be late for your next lesson. You're aware we don't allow loitering in the corridors." He added a clap which made the boys up their pace.

TO BLAME THEM

Once Sam and Bob set off after Mr Fitzpatrick, she glanced over her shoulder to see one of the boys, the tallest and broadest of the group, staring at them. He even had the audacity to wink at her. *Cheeky little shit!*

"That wouldn't be allowed, not when I was at school," Sam said after she joined Bob and Fitzpatrick in his office.

The teacher tilted his head. "I'm not with you, sorry."

"Three pupils wandering around the corridors when class had already started. May I ask why you didn't reprimand them?"

"I think you'll find I did just that, Inspector."

Sam's eyes widened. "Really? So, are you telling me that pupils rule the roost around here? Because from an outsider's point of view, that's what it looked like to me."

"I think you're wrong. Our way of dealing with the pupils might be different to other schools, however, it doesn't mean it is less effective, Inspector. Mrs Lowther prefers to treat the older pupils as young adults, not infants. Please, take a seat."

Sam noted how anxious the man seemed and continued to stare at him, adding to his discomfort. Her stomach was tingling with nervous energy, and she decided to go for the jugular. "Off the record, do you mind if I ask you a question, Mr Fitzpatrick?"

"I have nothing to hide. Go ahead."

"Do you believe there is an issue with bullying at this school?"

"Certainly not," he retorted sharply.

Sam continued to stare at him but remained unconvinced by his response.

She smiled. "Really? Okay, my observation after witnessing what has just occurred in the corridor, is that the pupils are a rule unto themselves around here, or some of them are."

"What a ridiculous statement. I categorically deny that, in fact, it couldn't be further from the truth."

"Is that right? Well, when I was at school, which admittedly was a few years ago now, I would *never* have been allowed to be seen strolling around the corridors with a group of my friends when I should have been attending a class."

"And that's not the case here either."

Sam raised an eyebrow. "Really?"

"Absolutely."

"Just out of interest, who were those boys?"

"Some of our best students."

"Ah, so they're treated differently, is that what you're saying? You allow certain individuals to push the boundaries?"

"Not at all. They must have had a genuine reason to be in the corridor at that time. Had I not been with you, I would have pressed them for an answer. It wasn't my main priority, dealing with you was."

Again, Sam was unconvinced by the excuse he had to offer. Instead of pushing the subject further, she relented and asked, "The purpose of our visit today is because we have reason to believe that the school has a disturbing bullying issue. Mrs Lowther denies that's the case, but we have proof that it's a genuine issue because over the past few months several pupils from this school have ended up in hospital. Are you aware of that fact, Mr Fitzpatrick?"

"You can call me Charles. Of course I'm aware of the incidents. What I'm not mindful of is that they happened because the children were bullied. Umm… we've also been notified that a student has lost his life this week. Are you suggesting that was to do with bullying as well?"

"In a way. Our sources have informed us that it was, however, from a different angle."

Puzzled, he tilted his head and asked, "I'm sorry, I'm not with you. Would you care to elaborate?"

"We believe that Leo Burke was a bully."

He gasped. "No way. I think you're massively wrong in your assumption. He's one of the brightest pupils in this school—sorry, I need to correct myself, he was—before his untimely death."

"That's as may be, but we have it on good authority that he used to hang around with four other boys who terrorised pupils from this school, after they'd left the premises. And before you ask, no, I have no intention of revealing my sources."

He bounced back in his chair. "Well, this is all news to me. Have you spoken to Leo's parents?"

"We've had a brief chat with them. Obviously, we didn't raise the issue about the bullying at a time when they're grieving the loss of their son, we're not that insensitive."

He ran his hands around his drained face. "I can't believe what I'm hearing."

"It's true. The reason behind our visit today was to ask Mrs Lowther to supply us with the names of the pupils Leo hung around with, here at school."

"May I ask why?"

"As part of our investigation we'd like to have a chat with them."

"Again, why?"

"I'm sure you can appreciate during an investigation of this nature how important it is to cover all the angles."

He frowned. "I'm still not grasping what you're saying. Sorry if you think I'm being dense."

Sam smiled. "Let me put it in clearer terms for you. We believe Leo may have been killed by the gang he hung around with."

"What? Why on earth would they do that to him?"

"That's what we intend to find out. There's a possibility that Leo thought about leaving the gang for some reason, and rather than let him go, the other gang members decided to teach him a lesson instead."

"Oh my, are you sure about this?"

"No, far from it. But it's an option we need to consider all the same. Can you supply us with the names of the boys he hung around with while he was on the school premises?"

"Did Mrs Lowther give the all-clear for me to do this?"

"Definitely. Feel free to give her a call."

"No, I'll take your word rather than disturb her. I'm aware she has several significant meetings this afternoon with anxious parents."

"Anxious parents?"

"It's the time of year when careers and the path the pupils want to take for their futures matter. Mrs Lowther always likes to offer a personal touch to the parents, to help guide them in their choice of which university they choose for their child's further education."

"In my day, that decision was down to the student. Are you telling me it has changed?"

"Not really. Mrs Lowther prefers to get in early with the children who have shone at school. She sees it as her moral duty to ensure the parents and the pupils make the right choice for the child. She's had a lot of success over the years. Helped several to achieve fabulous results. A few of the pupils who managed to obtain higher grades even got into Oxford or Cambridge. No mean feat, as you can imagine, not from a school of this standing in the community."

"I get where you're coming from, it's usually the pupils from private education who are offered the places, am I right?"

"Exactly."

"So that's the real reason behind Mrs Lowther denying or

refusing to conceive there could be a bullying issue at the school. She did mention she had a reputation to consider."

"Haven't we all? If people start bandying around the word bullying…"

"Don't stop there, Charles."

"Well, as Mrs Lowther has already stated, it can do untold damage to not only a school's reputation but also to that of the head and the teaching staff as well."

"But isn't that pushing the issue aside? Or brushing it under the carpet as I prefer to call it, instead of dealing with the problem? I have to be honest with you and tell you which I would prefer."

"As a parent of a pupil attending this school, I know which I'd prefer," Bob added after Sam nudged his knee.

"That's where different people's perspectives come into play. It's not always healthy to agree just for the sake of agreeing, is it?"

"I would have thought doing the right thing and keeping the other students safe would have been paramount to Mrs Lowther's reputation."

He shrugged but didn't respond. Sam sensed it was because, deep down, he knew she was right.

"Now, if you wouldn't mind giving us the names of the boys Leo hung around with?"

He sat there, just staring at her.

"Mr Fitzpatrick, did you hear me?"

"I did. Umm… we just passed them in the corridor."

Sam glanced at Bob and rolled her eyes. "We're going to need their names and addresses, if you don't mind?"

"I'm not sure I should do that. What will Mrs Lowther say?"

"That's why she rang you, so you could give us the details we're lacking for our investigation."

He tapped at his keyboard and studied the screen, then

the printer churned into life in the corner. He retrieved the printouts and handed them to Sam. "This is against my better judgement. Those boys are our star pupils."

Sam stood and walked towards the door. "That doesn't give them the right to terrorise the other pupils or attack them, or maybe it does, in your opinion?"

"No, it doesn't. I was merely pointing out the truth. I'm sure there's a reasonable explanation for all of this. I believe you're gravely mistaken, Inspector."

"I doubt it. Thanks for the information."

Sam flung open the door and stormed out of the room. She could hear Bob behind her, making excuses for her rude behaviour. She bellowed his name.

He caught up with her and tugged on her arm. "You're going to need to calm down, Sam."

"Why am I? I'm bloody livid that they've allowed this gang of boys to exert their brutish behaviour over the other pupils just because they're deemed to be the brightest pupils in the school. You witnessed the arrogance in those boys today and the reaction Charles had to them. That behaviour warranted a stern telling off. Did they get one?"

"No. Hey, I'm on your side, remember? What are you going to do now?"

"Have some lunch, I'm famished. Plus, I think we're going to need all the stamina we can muster later this afternoon."

"Meaning?"

"I intend to visit each of the boys after school."

Over a late lunch at a local pub not far from the school, Sam contacted the station and asked Claire to run each of the boys' names through the system. Given what Charles had said about them, she wasn't really expecting Claire to come back with any incriminating information.

"What does that tell us?" Bob said.

"Probably that the boys are cleverer than we anticipated."

"And?"

"And, it's going to be a privilege to knock them off their perch."

"Pedestal," he corrected her. "Good luck with that one, you're going to need to get past the parents first. If we show up at their homes, accusing the boys of bullying, the parents will be gunning for you."

"Grant me with some sense, Sergeant. We'll go in there softly-softly, to gather any and all information they want to give us about Leo. Then we'll hit them."

"And in the meantime?"

"We'll go back to the station. Head out again in an hour or so. What time does the school kick them out?"

"Three-thirty."

"Good, that'll soon come around."

CHAPTER 9

Josh was ready to mix things up a bit. He was fed up with hanging around at his aunt's house until she went to bed to make his move every night. No, today he'd go after more gang members directly after school. He was aware the gang rode their bikes to school and knew the routes they took. His idea was to punish two boys this afternoon and the final one tomorrow. Whether it worked out that way or not, only time would tell.

During his lunch hour, he had nipped back to the house. His aunt had been surprised to see him. He'd made up an excuse about leaving his homework at home and ran upstairs to his bedroom, to get changed. Leaving his aunt none the wiser, he left the house without saying farewell to the lazy cow watching *Loose Women* on the TV.

He'd hidden the knife and mask in the trunk of a tree in the woods close to the school, aware this was a risk, one that he was willing to take if it proved to be a means to an end.

The afternoon dragged. The teacher told him off a couple of times for not paying attention and forced him to read aloud part of the book they were studying as a class. He detested it being one of the classics. He constantly dropped his pen and skipped several pages on purpose, just to annoy the teacher more, hoping Mr Greenwood would choose someone else to complete the chapter. He chuckled internally and continued to plot how he was going to make two members of the gang pay.

FINALLY, after what turned out to be a very long afternoon, the bell rang. Josh took off like a greyhound out of the traps and made it to the tree five minutes later. He glanced over his shoulder. The main crowd of pupils were yet to emerge. He took the chance to take a breather and drank half a can of Fanta while he waited for the boys to appear. He spotted the three boys leaving the school gates together on their bikes.

Shit, I'd forgotten about them not being on foot.

He watched the group split up for a change. Was that done on purpose, because of what had happened to Leo? Had he scared the crap out of them by killing the idiot, or were they up to something? Either way, Josh was determined not to let the opportunity slip through his fingers.

He raised the chunky four-foot branch he'd found in the undergrowth that he suspected had fallen from the gnarled, elderly tree to his right, during the recent high winds that had battered most of the UK. Stepping closer to the edge of the woods, he watched Marco Falcon get nearer to his position. Josh was buoyed by the fact that Marco was wearing headphones so he doubted if he would be able to hear any nearby movement. Josh shuffled closer to the path and whacked Marco as he passed. The boy landed on the ground with a grunt. Josh hit him in the stomach again with the branch. Marco shook his head; he had no idea what was going on.

Josh ensured his mask was in place and jabbed at Marco

with the knife. "You fucker. How do you like it, eh, suffering a touch of your own medicine? Get up, I dare you. Come on, make a fight of it. Make my bloody day, Falcon."

"Who are you? Don't do this, I haven't done anything wrong. I was riding home on my bike, that's all."

"That's all? What about the rest of the week, eh? Or over the past few months? How many kids have you put in the hospital because of your bullying tactics? How many? Come on, I asked you a question, answer me."

"I can't. I don't know the answer."

"You screwed up, fuckwit. My brother was one of your victims. This is revenge for what you and your mates put him through." He jabbed and missed Marco's stomach by an inch.

"No, it wasn't me. You've made a mistake."

"Fuck off. I've been watching you and your saddo accomplices for months now, always had you on my radar but never had the courage to make you pay for what you've done to others, until this week. Think you can ruin other kids' lives just because you go around in a gang? You're wrong. Seen Leo and Aiden lately, have you?"

"Er… Leo is dead."

Josh leaned down and shouted in his face, "Yeah, I've got news for you, I frigging killed him. But I didn't get enough satisfaction out of that, not really. So, I came up with a more acceptable plan, to come after you bastards one by one and batter the fucking life out of you, just like you did to my brother. He's suffering in hospital. I'm going to ensure the same happens to you. I did that to Aiden yesterday, and now you're going to join him. Hopefully you'll end up on the same ward as my brother." He removed his mask.

"You!"

"Yes, me. I want you to remember this face and what I'm about to do to you for the rest of your miserable life."

"No, don't do this. I didn't touch your brother, it was Leo, he beat him up, I swear he did."

"How stupid do you think I am? I expected you to blame him because he can't speak up for himself now he's lying in the mortuary." Josh laughed and jabbed the knife again.

This time Marco cried out in pain as the blade sank into the fleshy part of his stomach.

"No, don't do this, please?"

Josh stabbed him a couple more times, just low enough so he missed all the vital organs. Then he dragged Marco back onto the path, ensuring he would be discovered before he bled out. Then he collected his belongings but left the Fanta can where it was and kicked it behind one of the larger trees. Bag in hand, he weaved through the trees to the estate on the other side. His intention was to catch up with Neil Parker; he knew where the boy lived. Hopefully he would have timed his journey to perfection. He waited across the street from Parker's house. He knew that Parker regularly stopped off at the shop at the end of the road for some snacks before heading home.

Parker appeared in his sightline, and Josh crossed the road and headed down the alley behind Parker's house. With his back turned, he leaned against the fence panel of the garden next door to Parker's. The bike approached, and the brakes screeched, bringing it to a halt close to Josh. He had the knife tucked in his jacket. The boy wheeled the bike past him, through the narrow gap, and Josh pounced on him, knocking Parker to the ground. Josh had no intention of hanging around to hold a conversation with the twat this time. He pierced one side of the boy's stomach with the blade and then the other. The boy cried out. Josh hadn't bothered to wear the mask this time, there was no one else around, so he figured there would be little to no chance of him getting caught.

He smiled down at Parker. "Remember my face, I think you'll be seeing a lot of it soon." He laughed and left the boy crying out in pain.

Dare he go for three on the bounce? Why not? He had time on his hands before he visited his brother. Rather than head off on foot, he stole Parker's bike. "Thanks, mate. I've had my eye on one of these for a while."

"Come back here. Help me. Stop thief!" he cried out pitifully.

Josh rode away, laughing.

He chastised himself a little while later. This wasn't supposed to be a game he was playing, this was real life, and he'd become a vigilante.

He knew the final boy, Daniel Morris, the leader of the gang, was going to be harder to bring down. Josh rode to Morris's home, a five-minute ride from Parker's house. It was on a new estate in Stainburn. Josh rode past the house first but couldn't see any kind of movement inside the property. He sensed Morris wasn't there and, in his mind, searched the local area.

The river, I bet he's cycling down there.

He pedalled faster than he'd ever pedalled before and reached the location three to four minutes later. His breath caught when he saw Daniel Morris. He'd stopped riding and was staring out at the fast-flowing water. Josh cycled up behind him and was tempted to push the menace in the water but stopped to reassess his plan. He'd located another wooded area a few feet back and collected another thick branch which he'd zipped up inside his jacket. Morris never saw the blow coming. He was knocked off the bike and stared up at Josh. They both smiled; Morris recognised him.

"I knew it was you who killed Leo and hurt Aiden. Come to finish me off, have you?"

"Nope, I would get no satisfaction in killing you. I want to continue seeing you every day, struggling to cope with the injuries I'm about to inflict. You deserve this, you're the coward, not my father."

Morris tipped his head back and laughed. "Arsewipe, you've always been a wimp, you haven't got it in you to attack me. We gave your brother a good walloping. Took it in turns, we did. He's lucky to be alive. If I had my way, I would have finished him off there and then, but the other boys chickened out, pleaded with me to spare his life, so I did."

"And I'm supposed to be grateful to you after that confession?" Josh withdrew the knife from the back of his trousers and climbed off the bike, which he laid on the grassy bank behind him.

Morris's laughter had dried up, and Josh witnessed the terror filling his eyes as he took a menacing step closer to his trembling body. The knife was prominent in Josh's hand, and Morris's gaze was drawn to the weapon. Large tears welled up, and one splashed onto his cheek. "Don't do this. My family are wealthy, I can get you all the money you and your brother need to start over again. I know how much you hate living with that aunt of yours."

"How do you know that?"

"I can tell. Let me help you get away from her. We can do it together."

Josh's lip curled. "I don't need anything from you. It would be blood money if you supplied it. Nope, not going to happen. You're going to lie there and suffer the consequences of your actions. You had no right doing that to my brother."

"And where were you? It was your fault we were able to get to him, you should have protected him. You're the one who left him in that vulnerable position. You're just like your father in that respect, you let Ben down."

The boiling blood tore through Josh like molten lava. He stabbed Morris in the stomach. This time he was so incensed by Morris's jibes that he didn't care where he struck. Morris stared at him and then looked down at the wound. Josh smiled and came at him again, determined to kill him, just like he'd executed Leo, going against everything he'd said to himself on the way to the location.

Out of nowhere, Morris jumped to his feet and ran along the riverbank. Despite his best efforts he didn't get very far. Josh caught up with him and stabbed him in the back. Morris hit the ground, face-first. He groaned and writhed in agony. Josh glanced up and saw a girl fifty feet away. *Shit! She probably saw everything.* Their gazes locked, and she shook her head and ran in the opposite direction.

"You'll keep." He spat on Morris and took off after the girl. His long legs caught up with her in no time at all, and he latched on to her arm and twisted her to face him.

"I didn't see anything. Please, don't hurt me."

His eyes narrowed. "Hey, I know you. You go to my school. Your father is a copper, ain't he? Milly, isn't it?"

Milly swallowed and nodded. "Yes, that's right. I promise I won't say anything, please don't hurt me. I know why you've done this. I knew it was you who killed Leo. If I were in your position, I think I would have done the same."

"Really? Even though your old man is a copper, you'd risk spending time behind bars?"

"Yes, absolutely. Let me help you get away. I can do that for you."

"I'm not going anywhere, not yet, not while my brother is still in hospital."

A man with a bouncy golden Labrador came towards them. Josh gripped Milly's elbow before she had a chance to run off. He dug the knife into her ribs and covered it with his jacket.

"Nice day for a walk by the river," Josh said to the man

who was now a few feet away from them, as if he didn't have a care in the world.

"That it is, son. Enjoy your walk with your girlfriend."

Josh smiled and watched the man continue on his route, heading in Morris's direction. "We need to get out of here. Scream and I'll kill you."

"I won't, I promise. I haven't done anything to you, please won't you let me go?"

"Not now, you're too valuable to me. You shouldn't have stood around watching, you should have had the sense to have hidden if you were that interested in observing what was going on. You're coming with me."

"Where? You can't make me."

He jabbed the knife, and Milly sucked in a breath. "Watch me."

Josh marched her back to the main road. He was on the other side of the town. *Where can I take her? I need to lock her up somewhere until I figure out what to do with her.* A light bulb went off in his head. He tapped his trouser pocket and grinned.

They walked for ten minutes. To anyone passing by they seemed like a loved-up couple. Josh had one arm draped around her shoulder and the tip of the knife chafing her ribcage.

"You don't need to hold the knife against me, I'm petrified enough as it is without having it rubbing against my skin."

"Ah, but it's doing its job, preventing you from screaming."

"Where are we going?" Milly asked, her voice quaking.

"You'll find out soon enough."

The house wasn't too far now. Another few minutes and they'd be safe, tucked away from the outside world. He mentally kicked himself when he realised there would be no essentials at the property, such as bread and milk.

I can sort that out later. I should have robbed Morris, taken all his money, money he'd probably nicked off the kids at school during breaktime.

"My feet hurt in these shoes."

He glanced down at the footwear she was wearing and laughed. "In trainers? Pull the other one. Stop trying to push my buttons, Milly, you'll be the loser."

"They're too tight for me. Mum was supposed to be picking me up some new ones."

"If that's the truth, tough. We're almost there now."

CHAPTER 10

Sam and Bob had spent a couple of hours at the station and were now on the road again, heading back to the area close to the school, their intention to have a chat with the parents of each of the boys they suspected of being bullies.

They knocked on the first door, and it remained unanswered. When they drew up at the home of Neil Parker there was an ambulance at the side of the house and a couple of patrol cars parked behind it.

"I don't like the look of this, and you know how much I hate coincidences."

"I hear you loud and clear," Bob replied.

They leapt out of the car and showed their IDs to the officer standing guard at the cordon.

"What's going on?" Sam asked.

"Young lad got stabbed in the alley, ma'am. He's conscious, just. The paramedics are dealing with him now."

"Do you know the boy's name?"

"Neil Parker."

Sam spun around and shouted, "Shit, shit, shit!"

"Do you know the lad?" the officer asked.

"Yes, we were on our way here to visit him and his parents. Any witnesses to the attack?"

"None. As I said, it happened in the alley out the back."

"Okay, thanks. We won't get in the way."

"It's tight down there, not much room even for the paramedics to work on the lad."

Sam and Bob took a few steps back towards the car.

"What do you think?" Bob asked.

"I'm not sure. Do we still reckon it's another member of the gang, attacking his chums?"

"Who knows? If he's not as bad as Haley, perhaps we'll be able to get some sense out of him. Instead of taking wild guesses about what's going on."

"Possibly. I'll try and speak with him when they put him in the ambulance."

"They're coming now."

Sam rushed forward. "Can I have a quick chat with him?"

"He's seriously injured. Are you his mother?" the paramedic closest to her asked.

"No, I'm DI Sam Cobbs. I'm investigating several similar crimes in the area, and I could do with having a word with Neil before you whisk him away. It could mean the difference between his attacker getting away or arrested this evening. Of course, it's your call."

"All right. One question and then we're going to hit the road."

She smiled and approached the top end of the stretcher after it had been placed in the back of the ambulance. "Neil, can you tell me who did this to you?"

He shook his head.

"Was it another member of your gang?"

"I said one question, out you get," the paramedic ordered.

"No," Neil replied.

"Thanks. Take care. We'll drop by the hospital and speak with you in the next day or two."

Sam's phone rang. She took a step to the side so the paramedic could fasten the back doors to his vehicle.

"DI Sam Cobbs."

"Hello, ma'am. I've got some bad news for you," Nick Travis said.

Sam's heart all but leapt into her mouth. "Don't tell me Ben Cox hasn't made it."

"No. He's fine. I've had reports of two boys being attacked. One in the woods close to the school and another down by the river over in Stainburn."

"Attacked? Can you tell me more?"

"Both the boys have stab wounds."

"Shit, okay. We're closer to Stainburn. Can you send me the location, Nick?"

"Sending it now."

"Are both boys conscious? Have they lost much blood?"

"I can find out that information for you and call you back."

"I'll stay on the line."

Bob was standing beside her, a puzzled expression creasing his brow.

She covered the phone with her hand. "Two further attacks on two boys."

"Do you know their names?"

She shook her head. "Nick's getting more information for me now."

"Are you there, ma'am?"

"I'm here. Before you give me any further details, do you know the names of the victims?"

"The first lad is Marco Falcon."

Sam groaned. "Another boy from the same gang."

"Ah, I wondered if it might be the case. The boy down by

the river wasn't really making sense when the witness found him."

"Is the witness still at the scene?"

"He is. He's really concerned about the lad."

"We'll drive over there. It's not too far from here."

She thumped her partner in the arm. His attention remained with the ambulance. Sam gestured for him to get in the car.

"We're on our way over there now. Good job there's no strike action going on at the hospital at the moment."

"I said the same," Nick replied.

Sam ended the call and hit the blues and twos. A crowd of people were standing in the road, gawping, blocking her way. They scattered once the siren alerted them that Sam was on the move.

She drove to the next location, and they followed the track to where the commotion was. The crime scene was on the riverbank, several metres away from the car park. The paramedics were already at the scene and doing the necessary to help the victim.

Sam flashed her warrant card at the paramedic closest to her. "How bad is he?"

"Bad enough. If you're wanting to have a word with him, you'd better make it quick. We'll be shifting him back to the ambulance soon."

"His name?"

"I'm not sure. He's lost quite a lot of blood. He keeps saying the name Josh, over and over, so I'm presuming that's his name."

Sam shot a glance at Bob. He hadn't heard the conversation, he was taking down notes from a man with a Lab sitting beside him. Sam presumed he was the witness. She crossed the path to interrupt their conversation. "Sorry, I need a quick word with my partner, we won't be long."

"Sure, don't mind me. I've only been stuck around here for thirty minutes or more, waiting for you lot to arrive."

"So sorry to inconvenience you. I promise, we'll be with you again in a moment or two." She tugged at Bob's elbow and steered him away from prying ears.

"Hey, what's going on? Is everything all right?"

"No, far from it. The victim keeps saying the name Josh over and over."

"Why? Is that his name?"

Sam chewed on her lip. "I've told you before how much I loathe coincidences and don't believe in them."

"You've lost me. Is that his name or not?"

"Don't you see, Bob? I don't think it is, I think he's Daniel Morris and he's trying to tell us that it was Josh who attacked him."

Bob ran a hand through his hair. "Holy crap! Well, this chap said he saw a lad with a young blonde girl walking back along the path, this way, not long before he found the victim."

"Could he give a description of the lad?"

"No. I asked him. He said the boy had his arm hooked around the girl's shoulders, but she seemed a bit uncomfortable. Her eyes kept widening as he walked past. He wondered if she had a tic or something similar, it was that prominent."

"Jesus, it sounds like he was holding her hostage to me. Maybe the girl witnessed the attack before the bloke came along and Josh was taking the girl with him... but where? Who is the girl?"

"Your guess is as good as mine. Hey, are you sure it's Josh Cox? Doesn't he usually visit his brother straight after school every day?"

"I'll ring the hospital to check." She tried the number several times but got the engaged signal once she was transferred to the relevant ward. "Shit, we're none the wiser."

"We could make our way over there, it's not too far," Bob suggested.

"I'm in two minds what to do for the best."

"I don't understand," Bob said. He peered over his shoulder at the witness who was stamping his feet on the grass. "He's getting restless, I should get back to him. Leave you to consider what we do next."

"Yes, go."

Sam paced the area while she focused on the paramedics dealing with the victim. They had transferred him to the stretcher now that his vital signs were more stable.

"We're on our way," one of the paramedics called out.

"We'll follow you." Sam had decided that would be the best option. She would leave it up to the staff at the hospital to contact the next of kin. Whether that was the right course of action or not, the urgency remained with her to check if Josh was at the hospital.

Bob joined her after waving farewell to the witness.

"Have you decided what to do next?" he asked.

"Yes, we'll head over to the hospital. Leave it up to the staff to call the parents. What we need to do is check if Josh is there. If he is, then we've been guilty of jumping to the wrong conclusion."

They started the walk back to the car.

"And if he isn't?"

"I'd rather not think about that just yet."

"I think you're going to need to. What if he was on a vigilante mission? If the victims were the bullies who put Ben in the hospital, then he's succeeded in bringing them down."

"But only one of them was killed, why?"

Bob shrugged. "You tell me."

Sam scratched her head and clicked the key fob to open the doors. "It's no good us standing here speculating, we need to get hold of Josh and see what he has to say about all of this. It could be a case of the victim throwing him under the bus, have you thought about that?"

Bob pulled a face and shook his head. "Really? He might be dying, and the first thing that comes to mind is plucking Josh's name out of the air, just for the sake of it?"

"All right, when you put it like that…"

THEY ARRIVED on the ward at five-thirty and spoke to the nurse on duty behind the desk.

Not recognising her, Sam produced her warrant card. "DI Sam Cobbs. My partner and I have visited Ben Cox several times since he was admitted. Is his brother here at the moment?"

"He is. Bless him, he never fails to show up. Perks his brother up no end when he's around. Sorry, I can't chat for long, we've been instructed to get beds ready for some new arrivals due in the next hour or so. Feel free to have a chat with the boys."

"Thanks." Sam wanted to ask the nurse more questions, but she could tell she was desperate to get on.

Sam noticed the curtain was still drawn around Haley's bed as well as Ben's. She poked her head through the gap in the curtain around the latter and smiled at Ben and Josh. "Hello, boys, can we come in?"

"Yes, that's fine. How are you, Inspector?" Josh asked. "Do you have some news for us about Dad?"

"Not yet. More to the point, how are you doing, Ben? It's good to see you have some colour in your cheeks today."

Ben smiled and wriggled to sit up straight. Josh stood and plumped up his brother's pillows.

"I had the best news today from the consultant. They're letting me go home tomorrow."

"Ahem... if you keep eating and taking your tablets properly," Josh added.

"How wonderful. You must both be thrilled," Sam replied. Discreetly, she inspected Josh's face and hands, checking if there were any bruises or scratches on them, or even possibly blood on his cuff or collar. There was nothing there. She took a step closer to Ben to get a better view of Josh whom she thought was avoiding looking at her for some reason. "Have you been here long, Josh?"

"I didn't check the time when I arrived. I came straight after school as usual. No, that's a lie. I stopped off at the supermarket to buy us a sandwich and a can of pop each because Ben hasn't really been eating the meals they've given him, and if he doesn't keep his strength up they won't release him. Any reason?"

"We've had a busy hour or so, after several pupils were reported having been attacked at different locations quite close to your school. Do you know anything about that, Josh?"

He frowned and locked gazes with her. "Me? No, I've not heard or seen anything. I came straight here and stopped off at the Co-op on the corner. So I left school quickly today. How terrible, isn't it, Ben? Do you know if it was the same people who attacked Ben? Is that what you're saying?"

Sam assessed both boys' reactions to the news. Ben had trouble looking at either Sam or Bob, but Josh held Sam's gaze a little too firmly, raising her suspicions.

"We'll leave it there and revisit the conversation in the future."

"You didn't answer my question," Josh said.

"Yes, we believe this has something to do with the attack on Ben," Sam reworded his question.

Josh nodded and smiled. "We'll see you soon. We both wish you good luck with your investigation, don't we, Ben?"

"What? Oh, yes. Good luck," Ben replied, his voice strained.

"We'll speak soon. Take care both of you."

Sam and Bob left the cubicle. She raised a finger to her lips, warning her partner not to say anything within earshot of the two boys.

They walked a few feet up the ward.

"He was too casual, wasn't he?" Bob asked.

"Far too nonchalant for my liking. He's involved all right. I'm wondering if we can ask security to check the CCTV for us, to verify what time he arrived. Can I leave that with you? I want to check how Aiden Haley is, see if he can tell us anything new."

"Okay, I'll text you if I have any luck."

"Do that, then we'll meet up back at the car. If Josh is behind the attacks, we won't be able to arrest him until we have crucial evidence to hand."

Bob nodded and set off. Sam stopped outside the curtain shielding Haley and cast an eye over her shoulder. She thought she saw Josh's head dip behind the curtain around his brother's bed, but maybe her eyes were deceiving her.

"Hello, it's DI Sam Cobbs. Are you there, Mrs Haley?"

A chair scraped on the floor, and the curtain was drawn back. "Oh, hello. Do you have any news for me?"

"Not at the moment, but we're working on it. I was visiting someone else at the hospital and thought I'd drop by to see how Aiden is."

"That's kind of you." She held the curtain open to reveal her son sleeping. "The nurses keep telling me it's a good sign, it means his body is in healing mode. Whatever that is."

"If they're satisfied with his progress then you should be, too. How are you doing? If you don't mind me saying you look exhausted."

"I catch forty winks here and there. I nipped home to

change earlier but I'll keep vigil beside him until he wakes up properly."

Sam rubbed her arm. "You're a good mum. Don't push yourself too hard, you might have a long road ahead of you. You should take this time to rest yourself and, yes, I know that's easier said than done."

"It's hard knowing what to do for the best."

Sam's phone vibrated in her pocket. "Excuse me, I have to get this. I'll say farewell, you know where I am if you need me."

Mrs Haley smiled, waved and mouthed a thank you to her.

Sam raced off the ward to answer her phone. "DI Sam Cobbs, how can I help?"

"Ah, there you are, ma'am, I was getting concerned when you didn't answer. It's Nick."

"We've had quite an eventful day, Sergeant, don't tell me you're going to add to it?"

"Sorry, yes, I am. I've just received a call from an estate agent. She was quite upset, took me a while to get the information out of her. When she finally calmed down, she told me she showed up at a house to do a viewing and was shocked to find a young girl bound and gagged at the property."

"What? Where was this?"

"That's the thing, you've been to the property recently, along with the SOCO team and the pathologist."

"We have?" Sam closed her eyes as the penny dropped. "Don't tell me it's the Coxs' house?"

"You've got it."

"Shit, okay. Here's what I need you to do. Send a patrol car to the hospital, that's where I am at the moment. I want the officers to come up to the Children's Ward on the second floor."

"I'm not with you. May I ask why?"

"Because Josh Cox is here. The final victim today whispered his name to the paramedics. We came here this afternoon to see if Josh was visiting his brother. Bob is checking the CCTV cameras to see when he arrived. Josh told us he came straight from school, only stopping off enroute at the Co-op nearby, to buy a sandwich for his brother."

"Gosh, umm... I haven't told you everything, ma'am."

"Oh God, what the hell have you held back? Come on, Nick, you know how much I hate not knowing all the information. Was the girl dead or alive?"

"She's very much alive and she's called Milly. It's Bob's daughter."

"Jesus, this is unbelievable. I need to find Bob. We had no idea she was missing. He's going to go berserk when he finds out. We've both said that Josh was nonchalant with us. I had my suspicions he was hiding something. Get that patrol car here ASAP. In the meantime, I'll stay outside the ward, make sure he doesn't leave."

"I'll arrange it now. They'll be with you within ten minutes, if not sooner."

"Thanks, Nick. Christ, I've just had a thought... all the victims are due to be transferred to the same ward his brother is on within the next hour or so. If you hadn't rung me, bloody hell, I dread to think what would have happened to those boys. Is that why Josh didn't kill them, because he had other plans for them?"

"Sounds like it. Christ, that boy must be really twisted."

"That's one word for it. I'll speak later." She ended the call and paced the corridor for the next ten minutes until she saw two uniformed officers emerge from the lift at the end of the corridor. She quickly apprised them of the situation and told them what she expected from them. Satisfied the task had been fully covered, Sam went in search of her partner. She texted him, asking him where he was as she took the lift down to the ground floor.

Bob's response was that they'd located the footage. Josh had lied, he'd only been at the hospital ten minutes before they'd got there. Bob was on the way to the car.

Winding her way through the warren of corridors to the entrance gave Sam the time to rehearse how she was going to tell her partner about his daughter.

Thank God Milly is alive. I don't think I could have handled telling him if she had been murdered. How the hell did she get involved? So many questions and not enough answers right now. But at least we have Josh where we want him.

By the time she met Bob at the car, her mouth was drier than sandpaper. She opened the doors and retrieved her bottle of water from the centre console and downed half of it.

"Thirsty, were you?" Bob laughed.

"Get in. I have something I need to tell you."

"Sounds ominous. Are you going to give me a hint what it's about?"

"No. Get in. Shit, I forgot to pay for my ticket. I'll be right back." She crossed the car park again, inserted her ticket into the machine and paid the fee then ran back to the car.

"Hey, you know I hate to be kept waiting for news."

"Have you got the footage?"

He rattled the disc in its case. "Copy in hand. I sense you're delaying. What's up?"

"Now you're going to need to keep calm. Listen fully to what I have to tell you before you react, promise me?"

He shrugged and held up his hands then dropped them into his lap. "Why do you always do this to me? Why can't you ever come right out and say what you need to say without all this shit?"

"I can't deal with this. I'm going to drive us somewhere

first and tell you at the other end, otherwise I sense the journey is going to be fraught and I fear I won't be able to handle you whilst driving at the same time. So bear with me."

"What the fuck? Could you get more cryptic? What the hell are you on about?"

"Just sit there and be quiet for five minutes, it's not far."

He exhaled loudly enough to match a raging bull. Sam hoped she was doing the right thing, keeping him in the dark until they reached the Coxs' house.

SHE DREW up behind the patrol car parked outside the property.

"Are you going to tell me what's going on now?" her impatient partner asked.

"You'll see when we get inside."

He grumbled something indecipherable and threw open the car door. Sam led the way into the house. The officer on duty recognised her and stood aside.

Sam followed the voices and opened the door to the lounge. Milly was sitting on the sofa, trembling. The second she laid eyes on her father, she flew out of her seat and into his arms.

Confused, Bob asked, "Mils, what are you doing here? Do you know the Cox boys?"

"It was horrible, Dad. I tried pleading with him to let me go. If that lady hadn't come in and found me… I don't know what he would have done to me."

Bob held his daughter away from him and wiped her tears away with his thumbs. He faced Sam and asked, "Will someone please tell me what's going on around here?"

"Why don't we all take a seat?" Sam suggested. She nodded for the female officer to leave them. "We'll be fine, thanks."

Sam sat opposite Milly. Bob lowered himself onto the sofa beside his daughter. They were gripping each other's hands.

"I'll tell you what I know and perhaps Milly can fill in the blanks for us."

Milly nodded, and her eyes welled up.

"I've received a call from the station telling me that an estate agent came to the house late this afternoon. The woman found Milly bound and gagged."

"What?" Bob shouted and shot out of his seat.

"Bob, you're going to need to keep calm. Think about Milly and what she's been through. She needs your support, not your anger."

"Again, you're talking in riddles, Sam. What the hell is going on? Why is Milly here and why in God's name was she tied up and gagged? Who did this to her? More to the point, why?"

"Milly, in your own time, can you tell us how you came to be here today?"

"I was on my way home from school, walking along by the river as usual, when I saw a boy being attacked by another boy. I tried to run, but the attacker came after me. I was so relieved when a man came along walking his Labrador. If he hadn't, I don't know…"

Bob's head swivelled between his daughter and Sam. "Wait, you were down by the river? I've told you not to go that way home, it could be dangerous."

"Dad, don't start. I've been going that way for months."

Sam tutted. "Let's revisit that another time, Bob."

"Easy for you to say," he mumbled. "Hang on a minute, we visited a location earlier down by the river where a boy had been attacked."

Sam nodded. "Exactly. I think Milly was the blonde girl the witness saw leaving the scene."

Bob's brow wrinkled, and he scratched his head. "Leaving the scene with whom?"

Sam inclined her head. "Think about it, Bob, where are we?"

It took a moment, but eventually the truth dawned on him.

He wrapped his arms around Milly and squeezed her tightly. "I'm going to kill the little fucker."

Sam resisted the temptation to smile. "No, you won't. Everything is in hand."

He released Milly and stared at her. "What do you mean? He's at the hospital, acting as if he hasn't got a frigging care in the world. Meanwhile, he kidnapped Milly, bound and gagged her and held her hostage. Remind me again why I shouldn't kill the fucker?"

"Because you know better than that. There are two officers at the hospital. He will be arrested the second he sets foot outside the ward."

"You knew about this and didn't arrest him there and then? Why?"

"I knew about it as I was leaving. After arranging assistance, I thought my priority should be getting you here to be with your daughter. Did I do the wrong thing?"

He shook his head and hugged Milly again. Over his daughter's head he mouthed thank you to Sam.

"Right, now you need to tell us if Josh hurt you at all, Milly. Do you need to see a doctor, get checked over?" Sam asked.

"No. I spoke to him throughout, told him I understood why he'd gone after the bullies. He didn't hurt me. I'm sorry, I can't be angry with him, in my opinion he's done the right thing. Those boys are a menace to society."

Bob held Milly away from him again. "Are they the ones who were bullying you at school?"

"Yes, and just about every other pupil in my year."

Sam noticed the colour return to her partner's cheeks and tip the scales to beetroot. "One thing at a time, Bob. We'll deal with Lowther once we have Milly back home and Josh locked up behind bars."

"He's a minor, he's done this intentionally, knowing full well they're not about to throw the book at him."

"I don't believe that to be the truth at all. We'll haul him in for questioning, see what he has to say for himself."

"There will be a certain amount of leniency, you mark my words, because of extenuating circumstances."

"We'll have to wait and see. Now, I think you should get Milly home or at least get her checked over at the hospital. What do you say, Milly?"

"I'm fine. I'd rather not go to the hospital if it's all right with you. I just want to go home to be with Mum and Dad."

"Shit. I need to give your mother a call." Bob excused himself from the room.

Sam slipped into his seat and wrapped her arm around Milly's shoulders. "Are you sure Josh didn't hurt you?"

"He didn't, I swear. While Dad is out of the room, I need to speak up for him. Josh went through hell at the hands of those thugs. We all know what happened to Ben, and the school refused to do anything about it. They're to blame, they let us down."

"Don't worry, we'll deal with the school. They won't be allowed to get away with this, whether Morris and his gang were the brightest kids in the school or not."

"They were. How could they do this? What did they hope to achieve?"

"Maybe they were bored."

Milly shook her head. "I can't believe that's true. Why be so cruel to the other pupils? None of this is making any sense."

"It will do, eventually. But that's not your concern."

"Please, Sam, I know Dad will try and do his best to talk me out of it, but I want to speak up for Josh in court. He was the only one brave enough to combat the bullies. Mrs Lowther and the other teachers have failed us. Josh shouldn't be punished, not when the system itself lets down the pupils."

"While I hear what you're saying, Milly, there are other things we need to take into consideration. Not only has Josh stabbed and beaten most of the gang members, but he also killed Leo Burke, as well. That's not something we will be able to ignore. The Burkes deserve justice for their son's death, don't you think?"

Milly's head dipped, and she fell silent. "What a mess, but none of this was Josh's fault, you need to emphasise that on his behalf, Sam. Promise me you'll speak up for him in front of the authorities?"

"I will, I promise. You're a very special human being to show such empathy and compassion to Josh, considering what he's done to you."

"I always try to see the good in people. I wonder how Dad is getting on with Mum. I think I'm the reason she walked out on us. I have a lot of making up to do… to both of them. My behaviour over the last few months has been abysmal. I felt trapped."

"You did? Can you explain why?"

"Because I couldn't see an end to the bullying. I tried to tell my teacher, but he brushed it aside, told me I needed to show him some proof. There was plenty of proof going on in the playground at lunchtimes, but the teachers turned a blind eye to it all. We were stuck in limbo, those who had been bullied by Morris and his gang."

"I'm so sorry this happened to you. We won't let the school or Mrs Lowther get away with this."

Bob entered the room. "Your mum is coming home; she's going to meet us at the house."

"Was she angry, Dad?"

"No, far from it, love. She was relieved you were safe, we all are. Is it all right if I take Milly home, Sam?"

"I was about to suggest the same. Go. I'll handle Josh. Get the officers to give you a lift to the station. I'm going to head back to the hospital."

"Good luck. Tell him if he'd laid a hand on Milly, he'd be lying in a hospital bed alongside his brother."

Sam smiled. "I'll pass the message on. Why don't you take the day off tomorrow and do something nice together as a family?"

"I'd like that, Dad, can we?"

He hugged his daughter. "I think a family day out is long overdue."

They all left the house. The estate agent was sitting in her car, and the officer outside pointed her out to Sam. She crossed the road to speak to the woman who was still visibly shaken.

"Hi, thanks for reporting the crime to the station. How are you holding up?"

"I've had better days. Is the girl okay?"

"She is. Her father is taking her home."

"Oh my, is he a police officer?"

"Yes, he's my partner."

"Is that why she was kidnapped?"

"Possibly, it's hard to know. We're going to need a statement from you in the next couple of days. Not now, I can see how upset you are. Go home. Are you okay to drive?"

"Yes, I think so. I don't live far, that's why I took the job on because I live around the corner."

"Do you have a card?"

"Yes." She handed it to Sam.

"A member of my team will be in touch, probably tomorrow."

"Okay. I'm in and out of the office all day. It would be better if they rang my mobile."

"Leave it with me. Drive carefully."

"I will."

Sam waved her off and walked back to her car. She removed her phone and dialled a number she had recently stored.

"Hi, Georgina. It's Sam Cobbs. Sorry to call so late, I need your help."

"Hi, Sam, that sounds ominous. What can I do for you?"

"Can I trouble you to meet me at the hospital? I'll fill you in when we get there."

"I'm on my way."

"I'll be there in ten minutes; I'll meet you in the reception area."

"See you soon."

EPILOGUE

Sam and Georgina met up at the hospital. During the lift journey up to the second floor, Sam brought a bemused Georgina up to date with what had been going on the past few days.

"I can't believe what I'm hearing. I would never have thought Josh would go to such extremes to avenge his brother's attack," Georgina said.

They completed their conversation outside the ward. Sam asked the officers on duty if Josh had tried to leave in her absence. He hadn't.

Sam sucked in a breath to calm her nerves. "Are you ready for this, Georgina?"

"Let's do it. I wonder what type of reception we're going to receive from the boys."

"I'm not sure, but with the other victims due to arrive on the same ward soon, there's an urgency for us to get Josh out of here in case things kick off."

"I wholeheartedly agree," Georgina said.

"We're going to need you to accompany us," Sam said to the two male officers. "I don't think he'll resist arrest but, you know as well as I do, things generally never turn out the way we expect them to."

Sam led the way onto the ward. There were two nurses on duty behind the desk. "We're here on official business to see Josh Cox, we'll be as quiet as possible."

"Shall we call security, just in case?"

"I don't think that will be necessary." Sam raised her thumb at Georgina and the officers. "Are we ready?"

She received an acknowledging nod from the three of them. They walked towards the curtained-off area surrounding Ben's bed. Sam drew back the curtain far enough so that the boys saw the uniformed officers standing behind her and Georgina.

"Hello, boys. Josh, I have reason to believe that over the past few days you have been on a revenge streak and attacked four members of a gang: Aiden Haley, Marco Falcon, Neil Parker and Daniel Morris. Do you have anything to say?"

Josh stood and moved closer to his brother and reached for his hand. "That's correct. They're the bullies who attacked and almost killed my brother."

"Am I right in thinking that you also killed Leo Burke?"

Josh shrugged. "I did. I was going to kill them all but then hatched a different plan."

"Let me see if I've got this right; you received little satisfaction when Leo took his last breath and you altered your plan to ensure the boys suffered long term instead, nursing serious injuries. How did I do?"

Josh smiled and squeezed his brother's hand. "You're spot on. I have no regrets. Those boys have brutalised the kids at my school for over a year now, and the teachers and the head have done nothing about it."

"While I understand the reasons behind the attacks, I can't condone your actions. You should have come to the police, to *me*. I would have helped you to get justice for Ben. You realise by carrying out these crimes you're now going to be separated from your brother for years."

"I know, it suddenly dawned on me today. I'm sorry. How did you find out?"

"We found Milly Jones at your house. She's now safely back home with her father."

"I'm glad. I never laid a finger on her. I had to stop her reporting back to her father what she'd witnessed."

"She told me. She also said that she'd be willing to speak up for you in court."

"She will? I know I went about this the wrong way, but I had to do something to stop them."

"I need you to come with me to the station."

Josh hugged Ben who was crying and clinging to his brother's arm.

"No, don't do this," Ben sobbed. "He only carried out the attacks because he was worried the boys would come after me, maybe kill me to prevent me from revealing who had attacked me. This is all wrong!"

"I know, Ben. But we can't have a vigilante society, that's why the police are there, to protect and serve. Josh, come with us, you will be arrested. Georgina will contact your aunt, let her know what has taken place."

Josh groaned. "She won't give a toss. She hates us. It was the worst thing you could have done, making us stay with her. She's lucky I didn't kill her; the thought had crossed my mind."

"Take him away, Officers," Sam ordered.

Josh went willingly and grinned as the officers led him away.

Sam and Georgina remained behind for a few minutes to comfort Ben who was understandably distressed.

Eventually, Sam sought help from the nurses, and they gave Ben a sedative to calm him.

"What are you going to do about the aunt?" Sam asked on the way back to the lift.

Georgina shrugged. "I'll put in a report. I'm not sure anything will come of it, though. I think it'll be a case of her word against Josh's."

"This has to be the saddest case I've ever had to investigate. Promise me one thing, Georgina."

"What's that?"

"That you'll do your best for the boys. I'll do the same. Between us, I think we can make a difference to what the future holds for Josh and his brother."

"Don't worry, I'm with you all the way."

THE END

THANK you for reading To Believe The Truth the next thrilling adventure is **To Judge Them**.

HAVE you read any of my other fast paced crime thrillers yet? Why not try the first book in the DI Sara Ramsey series No Right to Kill

OR GRAB the first book in the bestselling, award-winning, Justice series here, Cruel Justice.

OR THE FIRST book in the spin-off Justice Again series, Gone In Seconds.

PERHAPS YOU'D PREFER to try one of my other police procedural series, the DI Kayli Bright series which begins with The Missing Children.

OR MAYBE YOU'D enjoy the DI Sally Parker series set in Norfolk, Wrong Place.

OR MY GRITTY police procedural starring DI Nelson set in Manchester, Torn Apart.

OR MAYBE YOU'D like to try one of my successful psychological thrillers She's Gone, I KNOW THE TRUTH or Shattered Lives.

KEEP IN TOUCH WITH M A COMLEY

Pick up a FREE novella by signing up to my newsletter today.
https://BookHip.com/WBRTGW

BookBub
www.bookbub.com/authors/m-a-comley

Blog

http://melcomley.blogspot.com

Why not join my special Facebook group to take part in monthly giveaways.

Readers' Group

Printed in Great Britain
by Amazon